# On Duty

KETSIA LESSARD

◆ FriesenPress

Suite 300 - 990 Fort St
Victoria, BC, V8V 3K2
Canada

www.friesenpress.com

ISBN
978-1-5255-4036-3 (Hardcover)
978-1-5255-4037-0 (Paperback)
978-1-5255-4038-7 (eBook)

*1. FICTION, MYSTERY & DETECTIVE*

Distributed to the trade by The Ingram Book Company

# CONTENTS

*For my brother Eric*

# THE STUMBLING BLOCK
## (CONSTABLE NELSON)

I FIRST MET MY BABY SISTER AT THE Royal Canadian Mounted Police shooting range in Regina, Saskatchewan on June 10, 1999. Of all places, I never expected to find her in the Force, but nature can do extraordinary things. We had all gathered at the Depot Division for the Annual Firearms Qualification events when I heard she'd made it to the Fort Dufferin Cup Competition. It is difficult to convey the delight I felt as I read "Cst. Finlay, H. – G Division" on the board. An official RCMP headshot was the only picture of her that I'd managed to find so far, and I was desperately trying to associate it with one of these officers clad in identical earmuffs, eyeglasses and bulletproof vests.

Dozens of shots were fired, the paper targets brought in; only when the shooters' protective gear was shed was I able to recognize Heidi Finlay in a slight, dark blonde woman in her mid-twenties, just tall enough to meet the

Force's old height requirements. Her demeanour exuded little grace yet expressed great strength of character. She was accompanied by her detachment's corporal, a colossal Inuvialuk who had me stop dead in my tracks when the notion of walking up to her arose in my mind.

The Fort Dufferin Cup was awarded to Corporal Guy Dansereau from the Pukatawagan detachment that year. My sister did not make it to the Connaught Cup Competition, but she was no sore loser and shook Corporal Dansereau's hand with a smile. She left the room on her own, and I followed her discreetly. She had just exited the building when I saw her jotting something down on a piece of paper, holding the pen in her left hand.

"Are you ambidextrous?" I asked.

Heidi Finlay looked up.

"How do you know that?"

"I saw you earlier at the shooting range. You held your pistol with the right hand. And aimed with remarkable precision, I must say. Congratulations."

"Thank you. It's a cruel world for lefties. You learn to use the other hand as well."

"That's always impressed me. I'm Constable Jasper Nelson, Vancouver detachment."

She shook my hand.

"You work in the big city?"

"Yes. Not my cup of tea. I hear you're from Inuvik."

"I am. Have you been there?"

"I haven't had the pleasure."

"Some call it the RCMP's boot camp."

"Oh, I've spent many years in the North."

"Have you?"

"I was stationed in Grise Fiord ten years ago."

"Grise Fiord? Now, that's way above the treeline," she chuckled.

I believe I earned a bucketful of respect on the spot.

"...I know this is going to sound beyond strange," I began, "but I'm glad to finally meet you. I've been looking for you for over a year now."

"Looking for me?"

"Does the name Douglas Nelson sound familiar to you?"

Heidi turned pale.

"It does... Are you related?"

"He was my father."

She stared in a most uncomfortable fashion.

"He died?"

"Last year in March. He was very ill. I got transferred to Vancouver to look after him... He told me about you on his deathbed. He spoke of a letter your mother had sent him, mentioning your birth some nine months after a certain hunting trip of his. At the time, Dad thought it best to pretend nothing had happened and destroy the letter so my mother wouldn't find out. But it weighed heavily on his conscience in those last days. He confessed it all to me."

Heidi Finlay teared up and looked away. I could tell my words had rocked her world; her mind was trying to grasp and rearrange the pieces that would never fit together again.

"So, he did get that letter after all," she muttered. "I'd always wondered."

I suppose the young woman had entertained the flimsy hope that her mother's letter had never made it to its addressee, justifying her father's complete indifference towards her. The truth had filled her with shame. I was ashamed as well.

"Thank you for letting me know," she said, stifling a sob.

I believe privacy was all she wanted right then; she was about to walk away from me and all I found to say was: "I vowed to split Dad's estate with you if I ever found you."

Money was surely the last thing on her mind, but I succeeded in keeping her attention.

"Did he ask you to do this?"

"It was my idea."

"You don't know me. Why not pretend I don't exist and keep your money?"

"You're my sister, I couldn't do that."

"Is that how you look at it?"

"Yes, it is."

"What does your mother think of this?"

"I haven't told her yet. She'd probably say it's none of her business. They were divorced."

"I see."

"I want you to have it."

"How much are we talking about?"

"Two hundred and fifty thousand."

Heidi stared again, and the awkward silence was only broken by the sounds of tree sparrows frolicking in the elm above our heads. I asked if she would have supper with me, and she consented. We drove to a coffee house on Dewdney. She had wiped her face, slowly warming up to the reality that my incursion was bringing to her life. She didn't ask me to prove my story at first, probably due to the precise information I had provided and the noticeable physical likeness between us. Our genetics' feat had us both mesmerized. The RCMP headshot had not prepared me for this: Although my hair is lighter than hers, we share a jawline, amber green eyes and a relatively small build. A sense of connection was easily born out of this, proclaiming we were now travelling the same road.

I asked how her mother was. The woman was "doing well, under the circumstances."

"What circumstances are those?" I asked.

"What do you know about my mother?"

"Not much. Dad said she looked like Evelyn Hart."

Heidi had never heard of her. When her daughter was fourteen, Mabel Finlay had suffered a stroke that led to vascular dementia, making it unsafe for her to own kitchen knives and look after her family. Heidi once had to run for her life, so Ms. Finlay had been restrained and flown to a nursing home in Thunder Bay. Her sister lived in the city and had arranged for her relocation, which had caused quite a brawl. "She doesn't recognize me anymore," Heidi stated. Heidi had chosen to remain in Inuvik where a kind Inuvialuit family had taken her in until she was old enough to work and provide for herself.

Heidi wore no wedding band, and I assumed she was single, but I was wrong. She had a Métis husband, a Duncan Forrester who used to work as an accountant for a wealthy insurance broker in Inuvik. She had trusted him with their finances, unaware of his secret gambling addiction. Forrester had entangled them in a ridiculous amount of debt, and Heidi was left to foot the bill after he'd packed a bagful of valuables and left while she was out working an evening shift in September. She hadn't heard from him since. Their mortgage was foreclosed, and she'd just moved into a dead trapper's house on the outskirts of town. The modest building was close to the bush, which reminded her of the youth she'd spent on the trapline with her Inuvialuit guardians. Heidi had begun her career as a special constable, establishing a bond of trust between the Force and the Inuvialuit, as she understood the local language and culture well. She'd eventually been promoted to full constable but had been allowed to remain in Inuvik where she felt useful and appreciated.

"Are there any more of us?" she asked.

"Other siblings? Not that I'm aware of."

"How old are you?"

"Thirty-four."

"How long have you been in the Force?"

"Fifteen years."

"And you're still a constable?"

"I prefer the field. I love helping and defending people. Supervision is not my thing. I never asked for a promotion."

"Are you married? Do you have children?"

"I've had a couple of girlfriends through the years. But try to maintain a relationship when you're on call twenty-four hours a day, and you get transferred every three years. You know what they say: Out of sight, out of mind."

"Does your mother live in Vancouver?"

"She's a university teacher in Montreal."

This last detail appeared to intimidate Heidi in a particular way.

"What do you suppose your mother hoped to gain from sending that letter to Dad?" I asked. "Financial support?"

"Probably. She knew he worked for the government and was wealthy enough. Maybe she felt he had a right to know. Anyhow, I don't think my mother should be labelled as a victim in all this if that's what you think."

"No?"

"She did it on purpose. She told me so once. She loved her freedom. She was independent and didn't care for a husband. At some point, she decided she'd like to have a child of her own, so she set out to find a man who could give her that. She'd hit the town on Saturday night, looking for a drunken traveller who wouldn't stick around for too long. She found your father and got what she wanted that night. She thought I was a boy all along and meant to call me Cameron. She told me a few times."

"Did she make you feel she was disappointed you were a girl?"

"No... She'd sugar-coat the story when I was younger but told me the real tale later on. I never saw my mother in the same light after that. I understood she'd chosen to raise me without a father."

Heidi Finlay had experienced her fair share of hardships; what I couldn't tell from her attitude was whether she was jaded or resilient. I wrote a cheque for her part of our inheritance and handed it over. She examined the piece of paper and looked me squarely in the eye.

"If this is some kind of sick joke, I want to know right away."

Her tone had changed dramatically, but it was a reasonable reaction to a potentially life-changing situation. I showed her a copy of our father's will, my driver's license and my BC Care Card. The documents eased her suspicion. I also gave her a few photographs I had brought along with me. Heidi had never seen our father before and only knew him from her mother's vague description. She was curious but didn't know how to feel about the man. She made no comment except asking if I was the young boy in one of the pictures. It was rather late, and we agreed to meet again the next day. We talked some more. When the time came for Heidi and her colleagues to catch their flight, I asked if I could call her sometimes. I had managed to keep my composure all the way through but ended up crying like a child at this point. She was dumbfounded. She said I could call and let me hold her a moment. The indefinable mistrust I had sensed in her vanished that very instant.

We communicated several times during the summer months. It became increasingly obvious to me that I could no longer live by duty alone. The lonesomeness my lifestyle had produced had become a burden. The geographical distance kept my newfound sister away as well. I badly wanted out of Vancouver, and it dawned on me that a transfer to the Inuvik detachment was a viable solution to my predicament. I asked Heidi if she had any objection to this. She did not but was worried this transfer would strain my relationship with my mother. My mother is a rational woman, and I was confident she would understand my need. The transfer was granted. I spent a week in Montreal in August and asked my mother if she remembered the time my father had travelled to Inuvik for a hunting expedition in 1974.

"Oh yes, and he returned with that dreadful sheep's head I had to dust for years," she mumbled. "I could have burned it up."

She wasn't surprised to hear her husband had cheated on her during that trip, though I could tell she was annoyed. The reality of an illegitimate child born of this union came more as a shock. I had weighed my words with care, and my mother listened respectfully. She manifested unexpected compassion upon hearing Heidi's story. "I'd like to be of some assistance to her in her misfortunes," I explained. She nodded. I left Montreal with a certain peace of mind. But Heidi was right. An intangible wall had been erected between my mother and me; her calls became few and far between, and no effort I ever made could change anything about this.

I LANDED IN Inuvik on Labour Day. Heidi was on patrol duty and could not meet me on arrival. I took a taxi and made my way to my furnished house on Breynat. I was rather glad to feel the ground under my feet at the end of this seven-hour flight. Heidi expected me for supper, so I left at six o'clock and explored this town they call the "Place of Man". Humble yet colourful, the network of houses spread in irregular rows along the Mackenzie River reflected its residents' hardiness and fusion with the land. What Heidi had often referred to as "the bush" was far removed from what I had imagined living in British Columbia. I was used to lush forests and majestic Douglas firs, but this bush consisted of shoulder-high brush and long, gnarled conifers I later identified as black spruce. Tamaracks grew everywhere, turning to a rich ochre hue even this early in the season. I walked past the famous Igloo Church and admired the dome-shaped construction. A drunken Inuvialuk was lying on the church's steps, an empty mickey in his hand.

"Can I help you, sir?" I asked.

The man did not reply.

I found my sister stacking birch logs by a fire pit she'd built a stone's throw away from her old clapboard house. A moose rack boasting an impressive set of palms hung above the door. Heidi's hair was undone, and she'd traded her uniform for a tuque and fisherman sweater.

"Jasper, you made it in one piece!" she chirped.

I smiled and hesitantly wrapped my arms around her small frame. There was no reticence on her part, and I assumed the idea of having a sibling had grown on her as it had on me earlier.

"How was your flight?"

"Still wobbly on my feet. I hate sitting for so long."

"I just caught our supper," she declared, grabbing a gutted hare and lifting it high for me to see.

"That's fresh meat."

"Still warm, actually."

Heidi invited me in and led me to the kitchen. I offered to peel the potatoes and watched in awe as she promptly chopped the head and feet off the animal, asking me to help pull the skin off so she could dress the flesh for a stew of her own invention. I complied but soon lost my appetite. Heidi was so absorbed in her endeavour she did not notice my queasiness. She casually asked questions regarding my various postings, only pausing to wipe her bloody fingers and sharpen her ulu once in a while. To say I had not envisioned my baby sister as a butcher is a gross understatement. I felt relieved when the carving was done and the ingredients were gathered in a pot to be cooked on the open fire.

Daylight had begun to wane, and my hunger returned. I had not expected Inuvik's climate to be this cool in September, but the fire made it quite bearable. As grisly as its preparation had been, Heidi's stew was hearty and well-seasoned. I sat on a low camping chair and smiled to myself as my sister added wood to the pit to keep the flame aglow. She hadn't spoken much yet and had let me do most of the talking. She seemed distracted, and her unnaturally large and expressive eyes looked dull, betraying profound fatigue.

"You're thoughtful, Heidi," I observed. "Is there something bothering you?"

She shook her head.

"I'm quite relieved actually... I'm glad you're here."

"Relieved? How so?"

"I don't know. I've been feeling low lately."

"You still haven't heard from Duncan, have you?"

"No."

She told me the investigation into Forrester's disappearance had led the Inuvik detachment to some suspicious activity at Hall Insurance Brokers Limited, suggesting her husband's former employer used his business as a front. Solid evidence had not yet been produced, and Forrester's whereabouts remained a complete mystery.

"Everything you told me about our father forced me to be brutally honest with myself lately," she told me after this. "I'm not sure I really knew Duncan, but one thing I do know is that my marriage was a marriage of convenience."

"Was it? You didn't love him?"

"I'm not even sure I know what that means. He was the first I allowed in my life in that way. I'd always been wary of romance and kept every boy who'd take an interest in me at arm's length. I feared they were seeing something that wasn't there. I'd despise them for failing to understand what they were dealing with."

"Heidi, what are you saying? What does this have to do with Dad?"

"When I was growing up and having a good day, I believed my mother's letter had never made it to my father, but he'd like to meet me if he knew. Most other days, I remembered he was a government man who could have cared less about two lowlifes from Inuvik and wanted none of our dirt on his sleeves. When my mother lost her mind and my aunt took her to Thunder Bay, I did wonder if there was a way I could find my father. But I felt I had to prove myself to him. Joining the Force was a way of getting some standing, you know? The day I first put my red serge on, I felt ready to meet him. That uniform gave me standing.

Then Duncan came along. He had a mathematical way. He was an office man; he wore crisp collared shirts; he looked clean. He always looked clean. I liked that. Marrying him gave me more standing. I thought I was getting there. Yet, I often felt like a fraud under my uniform and thought someone would find out who I was and take it all away. And look at me now. I did lose it all in the end. But I don't care about standing anymore. I care about the people here, and I want to contribute. What they'll see is what they'll get."

I was deeply saddened and did not know how to respond. I kept quiet for the longest time but felt obliged to straighten her perspective so she would stop believing a lie.

"I knew our father, Heidi. I know for certain the reason he didn't reach out to you is panic and cowardice. It had nothing to do with your worth. It was easier to sweep the matter under the rug, and he did this with a lot of other things. My mother saw through his game, and their marriage fell apart. Sweeping those things away didn't make them disappear; they piled up high and tormented him to his end. He became obsessed with the idea of God's judgment and kept saying it was too late. He asked to speak to a chaplain in the hospital. It was after this he decided to tell me about you. The only thing I don't understand is why he didn't look for you after his divorce. I would have looked for you."

"Why did you look for me?"

"I felt compelled to. I needed to find you."

Looking for my sister had been like looking for a lost key; a sense of belonging with her had flowed naturally as if I'd been wondrously wired for it. This had not fully bloomed in her yet, and I wondered if it ever would in the same way. Anyhow, I was glad Heidi Finlay existed. In the first few months, my search had been fruitless, and I'd ultimately concluded Mabel Finlay had made this daughter up to obtain something from my father, which was not unlikely considering his wealth. I'd begun hating myself, thinking we'd fallen for the siren's clever trick; a profound disappointment had sucked the life out of me for a time, making me grieve for my father in a way I hadn't when he'd died. My foolish mind had even created this brunette child based on Johanna Spyri's character and my father's description of Mabel Finlay! What a dupe.

It was a whole year later that a suggestion from a colleague prompted me to call the Inuvik detachment to "put the matter to rest". I hoped a special constable who knew the town well could provide reliable information on the mysterious women. When Heidi Finlay herself had been referred to me as one of these special constables – except that "she's on patrol right now" – I'd nearly fallen off my chair. This girl existed in the flesh, and we shared a profession. A picture found in the RCMP database had revealed a perceptible genetic connection. Heidi was no longer a fanciful character but a missing piece of me. I don't believe I will experience this sort of elation ever again.

"People will talk," Heidi said. "They won't understand why you're doing this. They won't understand why you're willing to get some of that dirt on your sleeves."

"Heidi, we are not responsible for their choices. I don't see dirt when I look at you."

"Don't you? I see it. In more ways than one. Especially in this place."

"What do you mean?"

"Grollier Hall. The white man's intrusion. I was there last year when they took the priests to court. We had to protect those molesters from the crowd. The people would have killed them right there if they'd had the power."

Heidi was referring to a series of trials recently held in Inuvik for three Catholic priests who had abused children entrusted to them at Grollier Hall Residential School decades earlier. Four victims had committed suicide during the court proceedings. The white man's legacy would be brought up on a regular basis by the heavy drug and alcohol users Heidi arrested. One such man had spit on her the week before. The individuals she described sounded foolish and mean-spirited to me, but she took their words to heart. She felt the white man's dirt all over her soul and struggled to see how she could effectively right his wrongs.

"Some winter nights, it's like walking through a never-ending tunnel," she went on. "We see no improvement. The crime rate is going through the roof. A shift on the Saturday night drunk tank is enough to make you sick. What are we really doing here? What are we? White men picking up white men's pieces? Sometimes, I just can't face them. Even my friends. I wonder what they're thinking and not telling me. We broke their spirit, Jasper."

"I doubt your friends are holding you personally accountable for their pain. You're doing your best to bring them justice."

"Am I? Our efforts seem so inadequate at times. It's a cycle."

There was nothing we could add, and we both fell silent. The night had come, imposing its cold black sky and vibrant stars; I had forgotten how bright they appeared in the territories. The fire had almost died down, and I was worn out from my trip. Heidi offered me her couch to sleep on. The cushions were wide and supple, and I was soon dead to the world.

A rosy glow had lightened up the morning sky when an insistent knock woke us both with a start. A distressed Inuvialuit woman holding a child by the hand stood on the porch, and Heidi let her in.

"Sarah, what's going on?"

"Heidi, I need your help."

"What is it?"

"I left Aluki with my uncle Fred last night. He got drunk."

Sarah choked up. Heidi's eyes opened wide.

"She was asleep when I got home… I found her bruised with blood in her underwear this morning."

"What? Fred did this to her?"

"She says so. But someone else must have dropped by. There was no alcohol in the house; I'd made sure of it. He didn't bring any. The liquor store was closed… I don't know what to do, he's still lying there on the couch."

"He's in the house?"

"He passed out in the living room."

Muffled sobs rose from the girl's chest. She looked pale and forlorn and could be no older than five years of age. I wondered whether she understood the gravity of this conversation or if physical discomfort was the reason for her restlessness. Perhaps moral confusion had begun to seep in and dig its bitter roots within her.

"She's in pain," Heidi cried. "Take her to the doctor. I'll see to it."

The woman hurried away, and Heidi's eyes met mine.

"You know them well?" I asked.

"Aluki's my goddaughter. It was Sarah's family who took me in when my mother got sick. I need to go over there."

"Do you want me to come?"

"If you like."

Heidi washed up and jumped in her uniform. She adjusted her duty belt, and we made our way to a white house on Spruce Hill Drive.

"Where's Aluki's father?" I asked as we reached the porch.

"He's a bush pilot. He can be gone for extended periods, sometimes."

Heidi knocked.

"Has Fred Elias manifested abusive behaviour in the past?"

"No, Sarah would have never left her with him. I can hardly believe he would do such a thing. He has a drinking problem, like many of Grollier Hall's former students, but he has never harmed anyone but himself."

Heidi peeked through the living room window.

"Fred? Fred, it's Constable Finlay. Open the door."

There was no reply. Heidi knocked again.

"RCMP! Frederick Elias, you are under arrest for sexual assault."

A loud scream rang out, and a table got knocked over. We found the front door unlocked and walked in to see the middle-aged man run away through the back door. Heidi and I gave chase, following Elias through the street and into the bush. Some early risers watched from their porches with both alarm and curiosity. Elias whimpered as he ran. We ran faster, but he'd considerably outpaced us. His fast-moving silhouette soon disappeared behind a clump of leafy willows. The boreal forest provided effective cover and hindered our pursuit. We slowed down to catch our breath and look for suspicious movement and sounds.

We'd been hiking for nearly half an hour when Heidi stopped at the sight of a black scat on the ground. Flattened bushes indicated a large predator, and sure enough, a dark mass appeared among the thin birches beyond.

"A black bear," Heidi affirmed. "We're on his trail."

The beast of significant size approached at a steady pace, huffing and swatting the ground with its forepaws.

"We need to get out of here."

Heidi took my hand. We faced the bear and backed away slowly. My heart was racing. I'd once been confronted by an aggressive bison in the Yukon, and if an alert hunter had not intervened, I would not be here to tell the tale. I could not think clearly, but my sister was not so impressed. The animal exhaled loudly and charged.

"It's a bluff," Heidi said. "Let's go back to town."

"What about Elias?"

"I think I know where he's heading. The bear looks nervous, Jasper, I don't like it. We can come back later."

The bear followed us for a quarter of an hour, but we walked out of the bush unharmed. I breathed a sigh of relief.

"I've got to fill out some paperwork at the detachment," Heidi said.

I nodded. I remembered seeing an empty vodka bottle on the Kudlaks' floor. Considering the information Heidi had provided on our suspect, I proposed to drop by the liquor store and inquire about Elias' frequent bans. Unlike most of the Northwest Territories' communities which are either dry or restrictive, Inuvik has its own liquor store. Alcoholics can easily support their addiction there, but public drunkenness in the establishment can have them temporarily banned, forcing them to turn to bootleggers for spirits. The Elias case was about more than child abuse. I headed home, donned my uniform and walked to the store where I had a friendly chat with the manager. I joined my sister at the detachment an hour later. I found her talking to a stout man sporting a red moustache whom I rightly took to be our sergeant, Nathaniel Matthews.

"Constable Nelson?" the man asked. "You haven't started yet, and I hear you're already on a case?"

"It would seem so, yes."

"'Not slothful in business; fervent in spirit,'" Matthews declared, quoting Scripture. "I like it."

We shook hands.

"Did you find anything?" Heidi inquired.

"I did. The manager told me Elias is on a two-week ban for repeatedly trying to make a purchase while intoxicated. I don't believe he obtained his alcohol legally."

"Bootleggers," Heidi fumed.

Matthews looked at the young woman intently.

"Constable Finlay, you are close to the victim's family, I believe?"

"That's right, sir."

"Perhaps it would be wiser to let another member handle this case."

Heidi blushed.

"Sir, Sarah Kudlak came to me for help. I can't tell her to go hang. Besides, you keep insisting on this bond of trust we need to establish with the Inuit. I've been able to do so with both victims and suspect; certainly, this will be to our advantage."

"Watch it, Finlay. It's a delicate balance."

"I know, sir."

"Constable Nelson, can I trust you to be your sister's keeper?"

"Yes, sir."

Heidi cast a sidelong glance at me. She obviously did not like the idea of my keeping a close eye on her or telling her what to do.

A warrant was immediately issued for Frederick Elias; samples and fingerprints were collected at the Kudlak residence, and Heidi interrogated the mother about the incident. Sarah Kudlak brought her daughter to the detachment in the afternoon so we could proceed with questioning. I opened the interview room where the child knelt down on the sofa, holding a furry seal figurine in her hand.

"Are you ready to conduct the interview?" Heidi whispered.

"You want me to interview the girl?"

"For neutrality's sake. It's procedure. She knows me too well."

"But you're a woman. You should be asking her those questions. She'd feel safer with you."

"I can't. I'm an authority figure in her life. I might influence her answers. That's why Sergeant Matthews thought I shouldn't take the case."

I swallowed hard. Knowing the procedure was one thing; handling a case was another. I had dealt with this type of abuse before, but this was the youngest victim so far. I took a long look at the child; Aluki Kudlak struck me as highly introverted. How would I make her talk? And if I did, wouldn't a misplaced word break this fragile thing?

"Are you sure?"

"You have a kindly way. She'll feel safe with you; I know it."

"Should I approach her with play or drawings?"

"Don't beat around the bush. She won't like it. She's very bright. You can be straightforward, but be gentle. Sarah and I will have a little talk with her before you start. Let me get the recording equipment."

The camera was set, and Aluki prepared for her interview. Sarah and Heidi closed the door behind them but remained in the hall, keeping a sharp ear out. I sat across from the girl with a notepad in hand, introducing myself and asking her to state her full name. I hoped to project warmth and support but felt deeply uncomfortable; Aluki perceived this and stared guardedly. Her penetrating gaze followed my every movement to establish whether she could trust me or not.

"First of all, I would like to thank you for helping us with this investigation, Aluki."

My smile was met with silence.

"I am going to ask you a few questions about what happened last night. But first, I want to give you an occasion to tell it as you remember it."

A glint of fear appeared in the child's eyes. She curled up and faced the door. Shame was now associated with what had been done to her, and she squirmed as if she felt a stab of pain in her lower abdomen. I believe she was repulsed at the thought of a stranger knowing about her dishonour and having to describe it to him. Something had been torn from her, but she didn't quite understand what or why.

I could hardly repress my emotions, but communicating a sense of security was key. Through self-discipline, I assumed a confident tone: "Your mother left for a meeting last night, Aluki?"

"Yes."

"Where were you at that moment?"

"In bed."

"You were already in bed. Were you asleep?"

"No, not yet."

"What happened then?"

"I heard my mother talk to Uncle Fred and leave."

"After your mother left, did you see or hear anyone come into the house besides your great-uncle Fred?"

"No, I heard the TV. I fell asleep."

"You fell asleep. Did anything wake you from your sleep?"

Aluki looked out the window. She clammed up again and laboured breathing was her sole answer to my question. Distressing images and sensations tumbled in her mind as she tried to escape this inner chaos. Her silence lasted a full minute. But Aluki Kudlak's will imposed order and enabled her to speak:

"I woke up when Uncle Fred came into my room and took my clothes off."

NO CALL CAME to signal Elias' presence. Fingerprint identification confirmed the man's intrusion into Aluki's bedroom and no other suspect could be identified. Heidi and I were up early the next day, and we made our way to Elias' house on the west side of town. The brown building erected on piles had a plywood sheet for a front window. After knocking several times, Heidi found the door unlocked and walked in. She had never been inside and was not ready for the clutter awaiting her: the kitchen counters were littered with empty vodka bottles, and the floor hadn't been swept in weeks. Escaping reality was Elias' only concern; ignored responsibilities piled up and material possessions crumbled as intoxication sucked him into its blissful haze.

"This man's life is mere survival," I whispered. "Has he ever been married?"

"No, he's pretty lonesome. That's why Sarah's been trying to include him in her family life, you know."

"I don't think he's been in here."

"We can ask the neighbours."

"You think he's still hiding in the bush?"

"Quite likely."

We interrogated many individuals Heidi knew, starting with Elias' next-door neighbours. None of our potential witnesses had seen the suspect; none perceived him as a dangerous man; most pitied him and recalled his experience at Grollier Hall. A few residents were indeed aware of illegal activities conducted around town but would only provide evasive answers. My sister did not speak much. She observed and took notes as I handled the conversations touching on the abuse and the bootlegging operation.

"These people feel threatened, Jasper," Heidi declared after a moment. "I don't know what's going on, but it's worse than we think."

The liquor store was our final stop. I hereby hoped to obtain a major lead, but Heidi was pessimistic. A certain Daniel Smith was found behind the counter; my sister knew him well as a former classmate. A strange tension existed between them, and I discovered this Smith had nicknamed Heidi "Muskrat" and often bullied her about her teeth in elementary school.

"What's wrong with your teeth?" I asked.

"I have fairly large front teeth. It looked funny when they were growing out, so he thought it was a clever joke."

"He'd sure have noted the size of my fist if I'd been around," I muttered.

I didn't know how to approach the man now that I'd obtained this information. I tried to maintain a professional attitude: "Good morning, Mr. Smith. I am Constable Jasper Nelson from the Inuvik detachment. I was wondering if you could grant us a minute of your time."

"Sure," Smith replied with forced composure.

"The RCMP is currently investigating a bootlegging operation in and around Inuvik. We would like to know if you have noticed any unusual transactions taking place in recent weeks, such as a customer purchasing large amounts of alcohol for resale on a regular basis?"

"Bootleggers? You know how this works. They got their own tricks... They split up in teams and pay people to carry the cases for them; they say it's for personal use. I hear they even charter planes now. I couldn't tell who's really involved. They might just be buying for a big party, and there are no restrictions, so..."

"Could you still think of one or two individuals in particular? Anyone you know by name?"

"Sorry. I wish I could help you."

Heidi leaned on the counter and looked at Smith fixedly.

"You do know, Dan. Why don't you give us a name?"

He stared back as if her question was a trifle naïve.

"I don't want my house set on fire, Heidi. Can you understand that?"

Heidi was taken aback.

"Did you get this kind of threat?"

"What do you think?"

"Your deposition could be completely anonymous," I added.

"Yeah, like that would make a difference. If anybody snitches, we'll be the first ones targeted. We're in the best position to see everything."

"This is why you should do the right thing and tell us what you know. Bringing this operation down would make a difference for the whole Delta. We are trying to help, Mr. Smith, so you don't have to live in fear."

"God only knows how deep these networks go. I just can't take that risk. Bootlegging's part of life in the Delta. We might as well get used to it. There will always be good money in the dry towns. They can rake up $10,000 in a single weekend. Your fines are a joke."

I managed to contain my frustration, but Heidi was incensed and already walking out of the establishment.

"Thank you, Mr. Smith," I said after a moment. "If you change your mind, please give us a call at the detachment."

Heidi and I met with Sarah and Aluki Kudlak later that day to keep them informed about the investigation. Sarah had to run a few errands before her husband's hasty return. As we walked past Our Lady of Victory Church, Sarah stooped down and whispered something in her daughter's ear.

"Can we stop for a bit?" she asked. "I'd like to light a candle for Aluki."

We followed Sarah into the circular building. We sat down at the back where I counted twelve wooden beams supporting a ceiling built in the likeness of snow blocks;

the arches joined at the top where a stylized flower overlooked the entire construction.

Heidi told me about the Eliases' religiosity and how they had inculcated a sense of moral integrity in her that her mother could have never provided. Mabel Finlay had not been much of a churchgoer and was even less of a confessant. Through the Eliases' influence, Heidi had attended Christmas and Easter masses as a child and had passed through the sacraments. When Sarah had asked her to become Aluki's godmother, she'd begun taking spiritual matters seriously if only to honour her new responsibility.

Heidi admitted she hadn't set foot in the Igloo Church since the Grollier Hall trials. The trials had made her question her very faith. It had never been strong like Sarah's but had provided a foundation, a belief in an orderly universe, a true justice, an almighty God watching over all. No matter how remote Inuvik was in the world – "a few acres of snow" as Voltaire had scornfully stated – someone cared and could intervene if need be. She'd always taken this for granted, but this belief was wasting away and a horrible solitude had begun dragging her down the blackest of pits.

Heidi had mixed feelings about the Igloo Church. She'd often heard about the collective work that had made this construction possible – locals contributing hockey sticks to hold the structure together, and young Mona Thrasher deftly painting the Stations of the Cross as if led by the Creator himself. But what sort of hypocrisy was this? Our Lady of Victory was shaped as an igloo to celebrate the Inuit culture, yet this religion had worked so hard to trample it, plunging the people in deep confusion and leading them to self-destructive behaviour. What sort of victory was this? She dealt with the resulting high crime rate every day. She wondered how Sarah could embrace this God in the name of whom so much harm had befallen the Inuvialuit. She watched as Sarah helped her young daughter place the votive candle on the shelf. What would this abuse produce in Aluki's life? Would she try to numb the pain like so many others and consider taking her own life some day?

I FOUND MY sister leafing through a series of documents the next morning. I sat down by her desk and took a sip from my cup of coffee.

"Lab results are in," she announced. "Everything seems to corroborate Aluki's statement. I wonder how and where Fred met these bootleggers… I wish we could force Dan Smith to talk."

Sergeant Matthews joined us, a crumpled King James Bible under his arm.

"How's your investigation going, constables?" he inquired.

"A liquor store employee gave us some clues but wouldn't name anyone for fear of property damage," I answered.

"That's not reassuring… Is Elias involved?"

"We don't think so. He's a consumer."

"Any lead on his whereabouts?"

"There's a good chance he's hiding on the trapline," Heidi replied. "We were thinking of heading out there this afternoon and having a look around. I know the spot rather well."

"Let us know if you need backup."

Sergeant Matthews returned to his office. Heidi grasped a plastic container and handed it over: "You want some blueberries with that coffee?"

I reached down for a handful.

"You picked these around here?"

"I did."

A succession of mental images flashed through my mind as I chewed on the tart fruit.

"I had a vivid dream last night," I said. "I rarely remember them so clearly. I can't shake it off."

"What kind of dream?"

"I was here. We were giving chase in the bush. There were many officers involved and our suspect was elusive... I never even saw him, but it seemed like we'd been chasing him for years. He was causing a lot of damage. We could never get to him, and we were exhausted. At some point, I found myself near a lake, and there was a log cabin there. The door was ajar, so I walked in and saw Aluki. A man was holding her in his arms; her head was resting on his shoulder, and she looked peaceful. I never saw his face because he had his back to me, but I could hear him weeping. He was crying about what had happened to her and many others before her. His clothing was bright white, almost luminous. And I understood this man had answers, a solution to end our chase. He'd been there for a long time; we all knew about him but had not come to him or listened to him."

"Was that a real place we know? Someone we know?"

"I couldn't say... I saw one of his hands. There was a wound there."

"He was bleeding?"

"It was a scar of sorts, as if his wrist had been pierced all the way through."

Heidi giggled.

"Jasper, did Jesus appear to you in a dream?"

"Who knows?" I returned with a shrug.

Heidi knew most of the trails that led into the bush and had a notion Fred Elias was hiding in his brother Roy's vacant cabin out on the Dempster Highway. It was a long walk but a possible feat, so Heidi and I drove as far as the trails permitted. Our cruiser was left in a clearing, and we continued on foot. Vegetation was sparse, providing far better visibility than I had expected. I told Heidi of British Columbia's dense forests, and she listened dreamily, saying this is a place she'd like to see before she died. "I'll take you some day," I replied, and we walked until Heidi pointed to an undulating wisp of smoke in the distance. We soon reached Roy Elias' cabin. The cabin itself was a rudimentary assemblage of panels and planks with a thin stovepipe coming out on top. An outhouse, a cache and a smokehouse completed the picture. An extinguished cooking fire confirmed human presence; the cabin's lock had been forced, but Elias was not inside. The occupant had recently slept and found food there; soup cans had been opened and a Winchester rifle put to good use.

"He's been here all right," Heidi said.

We'd begun exploring the surrounding brush for sign when an uncanny silence filled the bush. Until then, ravens and chickadees had vocalized at will, and the breeze agitated the aspen without restraint. They were quiet now. My sister and I did not know what to make of it and were both filled with trepidation. Long minutes passed. The boreal forest gradually resumed its song. A sudden quiver in a yellow shrub had us draw our revolvers at once. A dark-haired man passed in a flash between two trees.

"Fred!" Heidi called.

The man scurried away, and we bolted in pursuit. Elias left the wooded terrain for a shady dirt road leading up to the Dempster Highway. I shot once in the air, as this will sometimes startle a fugitive and make him lie down for protection. Elias did not flinch. Fear is a potent stimulant, and the man proved surprisingly agile. I believe I heard him cry, "Leave me alone!" but I could barely make out the words. We were drawing closer, and Elias headed back to the wilderness for cover. Heidi was filled with vigour and determination to get her man; she shot several times in an attempt to stop him, but Elias avoided every bullet. I did wonder if she was shooting out of anger and remembered Sergeant Matthews' stern warning. We lost sight of the man once again. The search went on for almost an hour. We reluctantly admitted Elias had eluded us and returned to the cabin, expecting him to show up later for shelter. We found a patch of dry spruce needles and crouched down behind the bushes, agreeing to conduct a stakeout until nightfall.

"Thank God mosquito season is over," Heidi grumbled.

I began scanning the area at regular intervals using the small binoculars I carry in my coat pocket. Perplexed ptarmigans would land above our heads and fly away with a start as they noticed our presence. "That would make a fine roast," Heidi whispered, itching to seize her pistol and shoot. We shared some moose jerky she had brought along for supper, and I began worrying about bears. The day was growing increasingly cold; the sky darkened and the wind picked up.

"I don't think he's coming back," I said, feeling rather stiff. "He knows we've found his hiding place."

"I'm cold."

"Let's go."

We returned to town exhausted and empty-handed.

Our investigation was put on hold the following day as I was assigned to patrol duty and Heidi was involved in a substance abuse awareness campaign at the Samuel Hearne Secondary School. Corporal Alunik ventured back to Roy Elias' cabin, but found it empty; our man had definitely left the premises and found shelter elsewhere.

It was a quarter to seven when Heidi finished her supper and heard a huffing sound from her kitchen window. She ventured outside and saw a black bear moving calmly along the street. The animal locked eyes with her and disappeared into the brush. She'd never seen a bear so close to town and believed it was the animal we'd encountered earlier that week. She was relieved to see it leave when another silhouette emerged: a dark-haired man holding a weathered rope drew closer and closer. He looked down as he walked. Heidi froze as she realized Frederick Elias was standing right before her. The Inuvialuk stopped a few steps away from the porch. He dared look up a moment. Heidi peered into Elias' eyes to survey his intentions. She could only see shame and contrition there, but didn't feel an ounce of sympathy as she reflected on what Aluki Kudlak had endured and would certainly suffer in the years to come. Apprehension, disgust and pity intermingled in her mind as she asked: "Fred, did you come to turn your-self in?"

Elias repressed a sob.

"Heidi, can I talk to you before you take me to the tank?"

"I have no reason to trust you, Fred."

"I have no weapon. Only this rope I meant to hang myself with."

"I need to check you still."

Elias nodded and Heidi performed a pat down before throwing the rope away into the grass. She let the man in, keeping a close eye on him until she could reach her pistol. Elias was led to the kitchen. Heidi sat across from him with a hand on her weapon.

"What would you like to tell me?"

Elias couldn't find his words; Heidi's fear and severity greatly affected the impression of a friendly connection he'd once entertained with her.

"I wanted to say... I messed up. I know I messed up."

"You sure did."

"I never meant to hurt her, Heidi. Little Aluki, do you really think I would want to hurt her? I was drunk. I was not myself. I drink to get away from it all; it's always with me what they did."

Elias paused and covered his face with his hands.

"You mean the school?"

"...There are so many things you Mounties don't understand."

"We deal with this everyday, Fred. I think we do understand."

"You didn't have to go to those schools... It was Mounties like you who'd snatch the little ones away from their mothers. Forced them to go back when they ran away. Some died trying to make it home, you know. 'The scum' is what the nuns called us. Took our language away, made us ashamed of what we were. I know I did wrong, Heidi, but what I did to her, I had it done to me a dozen times. It was Father Houston who did it to me! And sober, too! The man of God! But I know he was no man of God; he didn't know the Creator at all. It was the Creator who stopped me from putting that rope around my neck. He had to drag me to the bush to sober me up and make me see the truth. He didn't let you find me until he was done. I know he understands."

Heidi lost her poise as a powerful surge of empathy flooded her whole being. The image of Fred sitting before her became a blur and disappeared behind a veil of tears. Heidi could grasp the cycle as lucidly as ever; she saw the Force's contribution to this dark legacy. Self-righteousness faded, and she listened humbly.

"You are going to arrest me, Heidi. And judge me for what I did. But will there be justice for me? Will you also judge Father Houston? He's out there, Heidi, you know it. He got out of jail easy. They're protecting him. He's still working as a priest in Manitoba."

Heidi looked down.

"There's only so much I can do, Fred, you know that. Some things are beyond our reach… I am sorry. I do feel the burden, you know. I know we are reaping what we've sown. Everything that's wrong with this town… I'm really sorry."

Elias sighed. He sighed as if he'd been expecting these words his entire life. I can't explain how Heidi pronouncing them could have this effect on him; she'd personally played no part in his affliction. Yet he recognized her as an

41

ambassador for her kin and received this apology like an ointment on his wound.

Heidi wiped her face and remembered her duty.

"If you want to do the right thing, you would tell us who those bootleggers you dealt with are. It would reduce your sentence. You know the kind of damage they can do here and across the Delta. They're making a thick profit out of people's misery. Everybody's afraid to speak."

"They work with Sadek," Elias declared.

"Adnan Sadek?"

"I don't know all their names. It was dark outside."

Heidi was considerably shocked; she knew Adnan Sadek as the hard-working businessman who owned the house with the fancy woodwork on Boot Lake Road. He'd moved in from Toronto a few years before, and she'd once accompanied him and her husband Duncan on a fishing trip on the Mackenzie River. Thick vegetation grew around Sadek's property, enabling the traffic to go unnoticed.

"You buy from Sadek?"

"When I can't help it. He keeps the stock hidden in his office. He gets most of the booze shipped to Fort MacPherson and Tsiigehtchic on the weekends but sells some around Inuvik too. Mostly on Sundays when everything's closed."

"Does he use unusual containers?"

"I've never seen that, but he doesn't have to. He's so loaded that he gets his own plane to deliver it."

Heidi drove Fred Elias to the detachment. They were about to enter the building when she took the handcuffs off her belt.

"I'm sorry, Fred, I have to."

She recited the arrest caution; Elias was cuffed, identified and taken to a cell. Heidi was discussing the arrest
with Corporal Alunik when I walked by and overheard
their conversation.

"Jasper, you're still here?"

"I had to finish up on my paperwork."

"Did you hear?"

"I did."

"Fred gave us a tip on the bootleggers. We got a warrant,
and we're going on a raid. We better get their stock before
it ends up in the dry towns on Friday. Clark and Alunik are
coming. We could use a hand."

"Let me get my vest."

I adjusted my body armour, and we left the detachment
in two cruisers, heading for Adnan Sadek's house on the
southeast side of town. Dusk had set in, and loud music
could be heard coming from the businessman's living room.
A black mini-van was parked by the porch. Constable
Clark inspected the passenger compartment using a flash-
light but found no alcohol inside. We cocked our revolvers and covered every exit. Alunik knocked. There was no
answer. The knocking intensified, and a young Inuvialuk
finally showed up at the door, his face turning pale at the
sight of our corporal's uniform. He attempted to make a
run for it, but Alunik grasped his sleeve and put the gun
barrel against his spine. He handcuffed the man, and we
walked in to find a second accomplice sitting in the living
room, his eyes glued to the television set. He was under
the influence and barely resisted the arrest, cackling away
as if this was part of a fascinating hallucination.

"Getting ready for a run?" Heidi asked, holding a mickey case she'd found in the office. "Where's Sadek?"

The men would not provide intelligence. Clark threatened the sober suspect at gunpoint: "Where is he?"

"He's gone hunting. He said he'd be back by nine."

It was a quarter past nine, and we hastened to lead the cuffed men to our vehicles.

Heidi found herself alone in Sadek's office, opening the liquor cases carefully packed for shipment. She'd begun making an inventory when the sound of footsteps came from the back door into the hall. Adnan Sadek walked in, a dead snow goose in one hand and a 12-gauge shotgun in the other.

"What the hell?"

"Stop right there!" Heidi shouted, pointing her pistol at the startled man.

A shot rang out. The back door was flung open, and Sadek fled into the darkness. Clark gave chase and followed the fugitive all the way to Boot Lake. The man was so desperate he jumped into the icy water. We had to fish him out before leading him dripping and shivering to a cruiser where he joined his underlings, still refusing to believe he had been defeated.

"Where's Heidi?" I asked.

"She's inside," Alunik replied.

I could not understand why Heidi had not pursued. I shot a telling glance at Alunik. We walked back to the house where we found my sister lying in Sadek's office, her left temple resting in a pool of blood on the wooden floor.

"He shot her?" Alunik asked, in disbelief.

My legs turned to jelly. I knelt down by the limp body, lifting and holding it without a sound.

"Finlay?" Alunik cried, shaking her arm.

Heidi's vest was badly ripped up under the neckline; a strange blend of fear and sorrow paralyzed me. An awareness came upon me at once: if Heidi Finlay died here on my knees, my existence would become vapid, and I could not bear it. Alunik called for assistance on his radio, but Heidi opened her eyes and stared in confusion.

"Did you catch him?" she asked.

"Finlay? Are you wounded?"

"He had a birdshot; he shot at close range and caught my vest. I lost my balance."

"You're bleeding."

Heidi wiped her forehead and looked at the blood on her fingers.

"I must have hit my head falling."

I sat down on the floor, holding my head with both hands.

"Where is he?"

"It's all right. Clark caught him by the lake."

Heidi rejoiced at this small victory.

"We need to tell Sarah."

"You need a doctor," I reprimanded, still shaken to the core.

"Later. Let's go."

Heidi was already on her feet and tottering out of Sadek's house.

"Small but sturdy," Alunik chuckled.

I was not amused. I got up to stop her, but Heidi knew a shortcut to her friend's house and was on the Kudlaks' porch before I could catch up with her. Sarah came to the door.

"Heidi?"

"We got them, Sarah. Fred turned himself in and gave us a name."

"Are you serious?"

"I'm dead serious."

Sarah noted Heidi's bloody forehead.

"Heidi, did you fight?"

"No, I fell."

"Come on in, let me clean you up."

"Don't bother, it's just a scratch."

"I don't want Aluki to see you like this."

Sarah took Heidi to the kitchen and washed her face. She took some raw seal fat out of the freezer and warmed it up before rubbing it into her friend's cut. We helped Heidi remove her vest and examined the dark bruising the pellets had left under her left clavicle.

"You need to get that checked," Sarah said.

A young Inuvialuk holding Aluki in his arms walked into the kitchen and observed me.

"Are you the brother from Vancouver?"

"That would be me."

"I'm Dave Kudlak."

We exchanged a firm handshake.

"You kind of look alike."

"Heidi, are you hurt?" Aluki asked.

"Your mom fixed me all up. I'm fine."

Aluki lay her head on her father's shoulder and put her arms around his neck.

"How is she holding up?" I inquired.

"Hard to say. She's not very talkative… She's been afraid to sleep in her own room. Been sleeping with us since."

"It's late, Dave," Sarah said. "She can't keep her eyes open."

Heidi stood up and pressed her nose against Aluki's cheek for a kunik kiss.

"Piqpagiyagit,"[1] she whispered.

Aluki smiled and waved as her father carried her into the hall.

Sarah took Heidi's hand and squeezed it warmly.

"Thank you, Heidi."

"It's not me. Fred had a change of heart in the bush, you know. I have no idea what happened, but I think your prayers were answered somehow."

There was a wry smile on Sarah's lips. Heidi shook her head.

"…I still don't understand why you asked me."

"Asked what?"

"To be her godmother."

"…I couldn't think of anybody else. I can see how love for truth and justice consumes you at times. I want you to communicate this to Aluki."

Sarah's words acted as a blow. Heidi looked away.

"Justice? You want a white woman to communicate a sense of justice to your daughter?"

Sarah was startled.

"Heidi, you know I don't look at you in that way."

I could tell Heidi had never discussed this load of guilt with her guardians, but her puzzling response only

---

1    Piqpagiyagit: Inuvialuktun for "I love you."

confirmed the righteousness Sarah prized in her friend. She wanted no distance to exist between them. Sarah pressed Heidi's forehead against hers.

I contemplated the beauty of their difference: Sarah Kudlak's free-flowing black hair against Heidi's fair locks secured in a tidy bun. I remembered why I had come to Inuvik in spite of the ugliness I'd witnessed in the past week. Perhaps the crooked could be straightened if there was repentance and a heart of forgiveness in the Place of Man.

Heidi and I stepped out in the chill of evening.

"Are you in pain?" I asked.

"I can bear it."

"You scared me half to death back there. I thought he'd shot you in the head, and it was all over. Be careful, Heidi."

"I wasn't being reckless, Jasper. He panicked and turned violent."

"This won't look good on his record."

"Are you heading home?"

"No, I'm taking you to the hospital."

"I'm fine."

"Heidi, I do intend to follow Sergeant Matthews' instructions."

"What instructions?"

"To be my sister's keeper."

"Good grief!" she muttered under her breath.

And I wondered if there wasn't a hint of a challenge in that exclamation.

# QITCHIRVIK[2]
## (CONSTABLE NELSON)

H AVING SERVED MANY YEARS ABOVE THE Arctic Circle, the polar night's dispiriting darkness is a phenomenon with which I am fairly familiar. But the first winter I spent in Inuvik began with an investigation much grimmer than the North's bleakest season. It was December the fifth. The time was 12:01 p.m. Corporal Alunik, my sister Heidi and myself had stepped outside Inuvik's RCMP detachment for a last glimpse of the sun before it set for a month, plunging the town in its annual period of complete obscurity. The air was cold but dry. There wasn't much sun to speak of, only a solar glow that was soon to fade away, but we needed those last minutes of daylight like a precious gulp of fresh air before a dive.

"You went undercover as an assassin?" was an incredulous Alunik's question regarding my unusual operations

---

2    Qitchirvik: Inuvialuktun word for both December and Christmas.

at the Vancouver detachment. "Why do I find that hard to believe?"

"It did happen. A colleague of mine who often posed as a gunman was out of the country when a woman called in to have her boss killed. My Staff Sergeant asked me to replace the officer because I fit the profile in this particular case."

"Did the woman request the angel Gabriel to carry out the job for her?"

"She wanted a man who looked harmless."

"That would explain it."

"How did it go?" Heidi inquired.

"We mostly spoke on the phone at first. She told me she'd tried poisoning his coffee before but the attempt had failed miserably. Our conversation was recorded. I sought to dissuade her, warning her of the possible consequences, but she wouldn't flinch. Her preferred method was a gunshot wound to the head. 'Using a silencer, of course...' We met, I showed her the weapon and she got really excited about how her victim would not suspect a thing. I faked the murder behind closed doors. We had two paramedics ready with a dummy on a stretcher who paraded around the office to convince her the execution had been successful. You should have seen the look on her face when her boss showed up, and she thought he'd been dead all along. I locked her up that very night."

Heidi was spellbound.

"Now, that's something I'd like to try. If I get transferred out of Inuvik, that is."

"Go undercover as contract killer?"

"Ha!"

"I don't think you could pull this off, Finlay."

"Bring it."

"We all know you've got the balls," Alunik said, "but… with a face like yours? Tell you what. If you ever move to Vancouver, I'll make sure you get to go undercover as a vegan activist."

"That's cruel."

The dim light was already fading when Sergeant Matthews showed his red moustache at the door.

"Gird up your loins with strength, constables. We have a case of breaking and entering on Nanuk Place."

We were immediately dispatched to the house of octogenarian Isaac Kaglik whose call had been cut short when a young thief knocked the receiver out of his hand. The assailant had fled with his late wife's jewellery and a tin box containing money for the Inuvik Food Bank. Mr. Kaglik was found lying on the floor with a nosebleed, broken ribs and a fractured wrist. An ambulance soon arrived; the old man wept bitterly, not so much from the pain but for the loss of his wife's possessions and the memories attached to them. Speaking the Inuvialuktun tongue, he held Corporal Alunik's hand, expressing his incomprehension at the thief's gratuitous violence and blatant intrusion. Heidi could only make out some of the words as the rest got lost in the intensity of Kaglik's emotional outburst.

I was left behind to collect evidence; Heidi and Alunik pursued the thief following a set of fresh tracks in the snow.

The culprit had been wise enough to wear gloves; no fingerprints could be found at the crime scene, but I took good note of his boot tracks. The feet were small, a size 6, and I wondered if our suspect was a boy or a man. I joined

Mr. Kaglik at the General Hospital. Medical personnel tended to the victim's injuries, administered an analgesic and settled him in bed. When he felt comfortable enough to talk, I sat down, pad and pen in hand, ready to jot down some of the information he could provide on his aggressor.

"How would you describe the suspect, Mr. Kaglik?"

"Inuvialuit. No older than twenty. He had long black hair, down to the shoulders."

"Any birthmark, scar or tattoo?"

"I didn't notice anything like that."

"How tall was he?"

"Not much taller than me. Scrawny."

"And how tall are you exactly?"

"Five-foot three."

The footprints led Heidi and Alunik to a scarlet house on Natala Drive. This was not their first visit to the occupant. This individual named Ken McLeod was a crafty drug dealer who managed to cover his tracks and use the law to his advantage. McLeod was unemployed yet owned a house at twenty years of age. His uncle held a trapping license, and McLeod had been known to trap as well, but he hadn't been seen at the Environment and Natural Resources office for the past year. We'd received phone calls from a neighbour describing unusual traffic at the red house, so a stakeout had been conducted to catch the dealer in the act. McLeod had changed his tactic, opting to meet clients around town where he'd been seen approaching teenagers. We expected a search warrant to be issued soon, allowing us to inspect the premises and put an end to his trade.

Alunik rang the bell. An elegant young man dressed in a charcoal suit and tie opened the door with a puzzled look on his face.

"Ken McLeod, what a pleasant surprise!" Heidi exclaimed with a sarcastic grin.

"What can I do for you, officers?"

"Your clients have a new game now?" Alunik asked, curtly. "Beating up the elderly and making away with their meagre possessions?"

"I don't know what you're talking about."

"Your neighbour Isaac Kaglik got robbed. Did the thief pay you in cash? Where did you put the loot?"

"I don't know any Isaac Kaglik. Do you have a warrant?"

"Not yet," Heidi said. "I see you fancy the businessman's attire now. You should open a shop."

McLeod shook his head.

"What day is it, Constable Finlay?"

"Sunday. What's your point?"

"I always attend mass with my mother on Sundays. I was at church all morning. Call and ask her yourself."

"I'll be damned," Alunik muttered. "And you fill up your pockets with charity money?"

"I don't!"

"We followed the attacker's boot tracks all the way to your place. What is he buying from you? Is he still here?"

"I'm alone. Nobody came since I returned from mass."

I'd meanwhile been busy matching Kaglik's description to potential suspects, and my voice came on the corporal's radio: "Corporal Alunik? I believe we have positive identification on one Jake Thrasher who was released from the North Slave Young Offender Facility last month. He'd been convicted for petty theft and drug possession. From Mr. Kaglik's account, I strongly believe Thrasher was experiencing severe withdrawal. He's right back at it."

Heidi kept a close eye on McLeod and noticed a strong reaction to the suspect's name.

"Drug possession? This is not looking good for you, McLeod," Alunik declared. "We'll see you soon. You can count on it."

Jake Thrasher's mug shot was soon printed on the cover of the *Inuvik Drum*. A warning was issued across the Mackenzie Delta regarding the offender's violent nature: "Keep your doors and windows locked at all times!" RCMP officers were dispatched to areas known for drug trafficking and all suspicious activity was closely monitored.

I was on patrol downtown three days later when I chanced upon my sister's childhood friend Sarah Kudlak and her young daughter Aluki; both were laden with heavy bags as they made their way to a black car parked by the Northmart grocery store.

"Sarah? Let me help!" I called, relieving them of their burdens.

"Thank you, Jasper... Are you on patrol?"

"I am. That's a lot of supplies! Are you planning an expedition?"

"Most of this stuff is for my folks on the trapline. I'm spending a few days at the cabin. I want Aluki to see her grandparents and learn about bush life. Heidi's also asked me to check her place to ensure everything's in order."

"It will be a great experience for your daughter."

Aluki looked up, down and up again, observing the ray of light emitted from a small headlamp fastened to her forehead.

"Is your husband out on deliveries?" I asked.

"He is. But he'll fly back for the holidays… I bet you didn't miss this darkness in Vancouver."

"Oh well…"

"At least there's Christmas to brighten it up," she said, indicating the colourful lights around the street. "Have you and Heidi planned anything at all?"

"We haven't talked about it yet."

"You are welcome to celebrate with us. Heidi spent Christmas with our family last year… She wasn't in much of a festive mood, to say the least."

"I can imagine that."

"Anything new on that thief, Thrasher?"

"Unfortunately, not. Either he's keeping quiet or he's left town, but there's been no sign of him these last few days."

"Is he from these parts?"

"Aklavik, actually. Heidi and Alunik think he's paired up with a drug dealer that they've been trying to nab for a while. His family has a cabin on the trapline. They went down there thinking Thrasher was hiding in the bush, but they didn't find him."

"I hope you catch him soon. Everybody's nervous knowing he might be lurking around the corner, you know."

Sarah fastened her daughter's seatbelt and sat behind the wheel.

"Ilaatnilu!"[3] I saluted as she waved goodbye.

---

3    Ilaatnilu: Inuvialuktun word for "goodbye."

I was home by six and cooking supper when my sister showed up at the door holding a large cardboard box.

"Jasper, I got that moose round for you."

"Oh, yes, thank you. Come on in."

I took the box to the kitchen and filled my freezer with the individually-wrapped meat portions.

"How much do I owe you?"

"It's on the house."

"Do you want to stay for supper? I'm experimenting with this black duck soup recipe."

"I'd love to. Do you need a hand?"

"I'm almost done."

Heidi hung her parka on a hook and had a look outside. This parka was made of thick burgundy fabric, and the hood comprised wolverine fur on the inside and a wolf trim in the traditional Inuvialuit fashion.

"You should lock your door with that rascal out there, Jasper," Heidi said, having found it open as she came in. "I know you could handle him, but you never know."

"I forgot."

"Maybe you should leave it... Turn the lights off, put something valuable in the window and lead the thief right to the police!"

"That's another option."

"Are you game?"

"I wonder what Sergeant Matthews would think of this method," I giggled.

Heidi looked around. Every room was still primer white.

"Are you going to hang anything on the walls? It's a bit plain."

"I should."

I hadn't spent much effort decorating, but the regular transfers had taught me to travel light and invest little time and money in what would soon be lost or destroyed.

"I could find you a nice set of antlers if you like. Or you could get some art from one of the artisans at the festival in July."

The only thing I had arranged with care was a high cabinet containing almost a hundred books; on the top shelf stood a black serpentine sculpture representing an Inuit mother carrying a newborn on her back.

"Where did you get this?"

"It was part of Dad's collection. Did your mother carry you like this when you were little?"

"No, she'd use a sleigh. What happened to Dad's Dall sheep trophy?"

"It was sold at the auction with the artwork and other valuables."

"That's too bad."

"You wish I'd saved it for you?"

Heidi shrugged with a smile.

"I hadn't met you yet. I didn't know you liked this sort of thing."

This was the first time Heidi had ever referred to our father as "Dad". I wondered if this came from hearing me use the word all the time or from new feelings emerging within her. The Dall sheep hunt had long been part of a tale she'd spun in her head about our father growing up, knowing so little about the man. Some pleasant childhood impressions were attached to that ram and to the hope she'd long entertained to meet our father and receive his love one day.

"You've read all these books?" she asked, running a finger across the spines. "It was quite a chance you had, having a professor for a mother, having access to all this knowledge… I wish I were so book smart. I should read more."

"Feel free to borrow any of these."

Heidi flipped through some of the volumes.

"Do you like being stationed across the country, meeting all sorts of people?"

"It's quite a learning experience. I feel lucky. But all this travel means you're constantly uprooted. Life becomes a succession of losses: losing your family when you first move away from home, being torn from friends and colleagues when you get a new posting, losing a girlfriend over the distance and the excessive workload… You get tired of it all. To tell you the truth, I dread my next transfer. I would like to settle down."

"You just got here in the fall! Are they talking of having you transferred already?"

Heidi stared, ostensibly grieved at the prospect.

"No. It's just a sensation I get from growing new roots again. I've met many officers who enjoy the change of scenery, crave it even; they hate to be stuck in a rut. They feel fine about having friends for a season and moving on. I find it hard myself."

"I can't say I'm too familiar with that feeling. I've always lived around here… They sent me back home as soon as I graduated. They knew I understood the culture. Or maybe they keep me here because no one wants to work in Inuvik anyway. Must be the mosquitoes."

The sound of soft footsteps and a body brushing against the door gave Heidi a start. She rushed to the window where she caught the glimpse of a long-haired man running into the street. For the quarter of a second, I thought I'd also discerned a face through the sheer curtain. We both stepped outside to investigate, but our visitor was long gone. When Heidi went home, she noticed a suspicious spider crack on her truck's windshield.

The next day, Corporal Alunik informed us that my sixteen-year-old neighbour had been arrested with 3.5 grams of cocaine in her possession. Another theft had occurred on Semmler Place, and Jake Thrasher's fingerprints were found all over the premises.

These events did little to help us stop our culprit, but a new lead soon put us back on Thrasher's trail. An old trapper by the name of Cliff Norris showed up at the detachment, ready to haul the burglar over the coals. Norris claimed Jake Thrasher had stolen a sackful of pelts he'd loaded unto his truck to sell at the Environment and Natural Resource office. He believed he'd seen Jake Thrasher sitting on a stump across the road as he'd carried the pelts to his vehicle. When he'd turned around to get a closer look, the young man had disappeared. Norris had gone back to fetch his bag. He'd only noticed the missing bundle once he'd reached the ENR office.

"Could you provide a list of the stolen pelts?" Alunik asked.

"I sure could. It was all marten fur, but there was a wolverine and a white fox in the lot, so I believe it could easily be recognized."

"We will contact the office immediately."

"Are you certain this was Jake Thrasher?" I asked.

"It was a little guy. He wore jeans and a black coat. It was the face I saw in the paper last week."

A closer investigation revealed Thrasher's familiar boot tracks around Norris' front porch. As frustrating as this loss was for the trapper who'd worked hard fleshing and stretching his pelts, we knew Thrasher's game was almost up as the bundle would likely be recovered; there was no way he could get payment but to go through the ENR office.

The pelt theft took a surprising turn when a Gwich'in girl was found beaten and unconscious in the cemetery around suppertime. Heidi had just arrived at the detachment for her evening shift when she was accosted by Sergeant Matthews on his way out of the office.

"Constable Finlay! There's a development regarding the Thrasher case. We have another assault victim. I need you to go to the hospital and take her statement. She just came to and she's ready to talk."

"A new victim? Who is she?"

"Fourteen-year-old Clara Snowshoe, room 31. She was found half-buried in the snow by a passer-by in the cemetery. She was suffering from severe hypothermia. Corporal Alunik gathered some evidence on location and identified Thrasher's boot tracks again."

Heidi found the girl lying on her hospital bed, her mother sitting by her side holding her hand. With a considerably hoarse voice, the weak adolescent revealed some details confirming Thrasher's link to the pelt theft: "I stopped by the cemetery to visit my grandfather's grave," she began. "A little man with a wolverine pelt on his head walked by and stopped a few steps away from me. At first,

I didn't know what I was looking at, so I stared a long time. He was waiting for someone. At one point, he turned around and noticed me. I'd seen his face on the news and recognized him right away. I panicked and tried to run, but he chased me and grabbed me from behind. He strangled me until I passed out.

"I came back to my senses a while later. I heard him talking to another man who asked him: 'Is that a dead girl?'

"He was piling up a whole bunch of snow over me. The little man replied: 'I don't think she's dead… I had to, she was going to tell on me.' He said: 'You've got to help me out, man. Why can't you let me stay at your cabin?' The other guy said he had 'the Grizzly and the bastard Mountie' breathing down his neck and couldn't take chances. The little man noticed I'd woken up and hit me on the head. I don't remember anything after that."

Heidi pressed Clara Snowshoe for more details about the accomplice and his car, but the dim light and the heavy outerwear had prevented her from getting a clear picture. "I think it was a white guy," she said. "His car was some shade of grey."

Would Jake Thrasher dare show his face at the ENR counter and try to get paid for the work he hadn't done? Would the accomplice be soon revealed? We were not particularly surprised to hear from the office two days later of "one Ken McLeod who's handed us what appears to be Cliff Norris' pelts using his uncle's licence." Corporal Alunik got the tip and immediately dispatched Heidi and I to the establishment.

As soon as the wary clerk had turned away to make the call, McLeod had known he could no longer deny his connection to Thrasher. He'd abandoned the pelts and run like the wind. We met him by the front door. The sight of our uniforms put a new spring in his step: McLeod headed straight for the spruce grove bordering the building, and we followed him closely. Our uniforms and heavy equipment slowed us down, but I managed to catch up with the man and almost grasped his sleeve. McLeod yelped. The woodlot ended. We found ourselves on Gwich'in Road, where our offender found a hiding spot at a nearby house, and we lost him in the dark. The owners kept their snowmobile in the backyard and had been careless enough to leave the key in the ignition, a common enough mistake in the North. McLeod did not think twice. He straddled the vehicle and rode into the bush, leaving us both panting in the street.

I suppose Ken McLeod's initial impression was one of relief and satisfaction. But as he penetrated the darkness' nether regions, it surely occurred to him that he would now have to hide and cut himself off from light and society. He had been wading in murky waters for months, managing to lie to himself about the nature of his lucrative business. But like Thrasher, he was a thief; not only because of the snowmobile, but because he stole lives for a living, making slaves out of youngsters hungry for a trip or thirsting after any substance to numb the pain, even for a short while. As he made his way to the trapline, McLeod gave up and entered the survival cycle.

MY SISTER AND I were put on highway patrol the following day. I was running late and found Heidi waiting at the wheel, ensuring the radar and radio systems worked properly. I sat down shivering from head to toe, my fur hat's flaps fastened tightly underneath my chin.

"May I?" I asked, turning the cruiser's heat up.

"Go ahead. It's a bit brisk today, eh?"

"My boiler broke down."

"No way!"

"It was a rude awakening this morning. But I called a repairman, and it should be fixed soon."

"I hope so. You are rather fond of that hat, aren't you?"

"I appreciate its warmth. I believe Vancouver's mild winters have spoiled me."

"How cold does it get in Grise Fiord?"

"Fifty below is the worst I've seen. But the average is around thirty."

"Only thirty below? That's the good life."

This was the second time I'd been put on highway patrol with Heidi as a partner since I'd been transferred to the Inuvik detachment. The ice road over the Mackenzie River had recently opened to larger vehicles, and my sister expected important truck traffic on the Dempster with shipments moving to and from Dawson after a long wait for the freeze-up. We soon encountered an immobilized vehicle with a flat tire, a regular occurrence on this bumpy gravel road. The driver, a robust lady in her fifties, said she did not need our help, but I insisted, and she was rather grateful in the end: "Beat it now, Heidi. Go help the folks who could really use a hand, not old Maureen who's patched dozens of tires in her sorry lifetime."

We did encounter a good number of eighteen-wheelers heading to Inuvik and had to stop an impaired driver on his way to Dawson, a few kilometres away from the frozen river. The drive back to the detachment was long enough, and I was puzzled at how quiet our young offender was as he'd been rough and rebellious upon arrest. Heidi and I had been discussing raw meat before. After hearing of my disgust for seal flesh's ferrous taste, she soon resumed our talk, declaring beluga maktak wasn't bad, but she hadn't had any in a long while. She preferred the taste of caribou quak, that is raw meat frozen and eaten as is. She reminisced about a hunting trip Roy Elias had taken her on as a teenager, teaching her how to skin the animal and cut it up for packing: "You start right above the tail and cut along the spine. Incisions on each side of the neck and above the legs will make the skin come right off with a few strong pulls. The head needs to come off next and that means deep cuts all around, and then you twist it using the antlers. The whole thing snaps, and you can remove it easily."

"I need to stop," our passenger moaned.

I turned around and noticed how green his face looked. Heidi hit the brakes, and I only had time to open the door so the drunk could regurgitate on the curb. I suggested she drop the subject.

"Are you a Southerner?" she asked.

"I'm from Toronto, ma'am."

Heidi went on to praise the work of one George Roberts, a gifted knifemaker from Whitehorse who'd sold her a thick skinning blade at the Great Northern Arts Festival the year before. Roberts used surgical steel and his knives could cut right through the bone. It was a trustworthy tool, and she always carried it on her when she was out in the bush. Our offender was quite compliant when we reached the detachment. I believe my sister left a lasting impression on him. I'd gotten more or less used to Heidi's graphic tales and was agreeably surprised to hear her light-hearted chat as she can be quiet and hard to read at times.

Until then, my profession as a RCMP officer had never given me the sort of satisfaction I felt working in Inuvik. I'd been blessed with genial colleagues through the years, but this new partnership provided a deeper, more permanent sort of bond. The distinct yet absurd notion that spending time with Heidi Finlay brought me back to childhood persisted as pleasant moods and memories rushed back in waves: tobogganing down Parker hill with my friends; a game of hide and seek in the dark; building a snow fort in the backyard; playing hockey late into the night, my carefree self losing track of time as I savoured the simple joy of companionship. My sister had not been part of these moments, but her presence brought me a similar plenitude. I was amazed to get a taste of this after so many years, as I believed this state of mind to belong to a time of innocence when boundless expectations make delights fuller and perhaps even exaggerated.

We issued a few speeding tickets and stopped for lunch near the Richardson Mountains. We dined on smoked char sandwiches, black tea and blueberry muffins Heidi had baked and frozen in the fall. The mountain range, magnificent in its autumn colours, was now a series of ominous masses under December's blue shadows; an uneasy sense of vulnerability had replaced the awe and freedom the vista usually inspires. We were about to resume our patrol when a lone Dall ram crossed the highway and stopped before our cruiser. The white animal stared in the most unusual fashion, its solid curling horns pointing nobly towards the sky. Heidi was in a sort of trance. She stepped onto the road and gingerly approached the ram. I wondered if her plan was to turn it into a trophy, but no, she only stretched out her hand and touched the animal's head before it scampered away into the mountains.

We were approaching town in the afternoon when I remembered an envelope I'd stuffed in my coat pocket upon leaving the detachment.

"I found this on my desk."

"It's Sergeant Matthews' Christmas card. He hands them out early."

I opened the envelope and pulled out a greeting card representing the Nativity in a stained-glass window.

"What Scripture did you get?"

"'He hath delivered us from the power of darkness, and hath translated us into the kingdom of his dear Son.'"

"So full of Christmas cheer!"

"What did you get?"

"Something about people dwelling in the land of the shadow of death seeing a great light."

"Does it get to you?"

"What?"

"This everlasting night."

"Last year it did. Badly."

"Because of your husband's flight?"

Heidi nodded.

"There's something mysterious and even soothing about the darkness at first. But it always overwhelms you in the end."

"I hear dealers and bootleggers have a name for you now."

"The 'bastard Mountie'? Yes, I heard… I knew people would talk. One of them called me that to my face from his cell the other day. Alunik told him to watch his tongue. When he brought his meal, he'd poured half a bottle of Tabasco into his food."

"He did? Get out!"

"Yes, he did."

"I owe him one for this!"

Heidi had a vague smile.

"You don't like it."

"How would you feel?"

With all her grit, I would have thought crude insults about my sister's illegitimate conception would have slipped like water off a duck's back. Heidi was not amused. I laid a hand on the back of her neck and squeezed it gently.

"You know what that means, though. The underworld fears you. You must be doing something right."

"It's still mean."

"I know."

Heidi had always carried a load of shame inherited by no fault of her own, but my arrival in Inuvik had revived the locals' curiosity. Gaining a half-brother meant making her begetters' sin public domain. Seeing how news had spread like wildfire, Heidi had concluded that many whom she considered friends were really deceitful gossips who had added colours and details to the story she'd rather not hear herself.

"It hurts me too," I said, after a moment. "I don't want them to insult you."

Heidi did not reply.

"Do you sometimes wish Dad had died with his secret?"

"No. I wouldn't know the truth, and we'd still be apart. I'd rather put up with the consequences."

"Things could have been so different. I feel robbed when I think about it. I feel robbed that no one told me when you were born. I didn't get to hold you. That would have been meaningful to me."

"It's done now," Heidi said softly.

"I know."

A black car driving in the opposite direction interrupted our conversation as it flashed its headlights at us.

"We are needed," I said.

"Isn't that Sarah's car?"

"Might be."

The car stopped by the wayside, and Sarah Kudlak stepped out, frantically waving her arms at us. Heidi immobilized the cruiser.

"I thought I'd find you out here at this time of day," the woman said, visibly agitated. "Jake Thrasher's on the trapline."

"You've seen Thrasher?"

"You're not going to like this. He broke into your cabin, and he's squatting there with a friend right now. They have a snowmobile. They looked kind of high to me, so I think there might be drugs involved."

"What a madcap!" Heidi snapped. "Is this friend Ken McLeod?"

"I don't know his name, but I've seen him in church."

"Twenty-something Caucasian, medium build, light brown hair, crew cut."

"He would fit that description."

"A personal attack, you think?" I asked. "Does he know where your cabin is?"

"I think he does."

"Get back to your lodge and lock yourself up with your family, Sarah," I said. "Thrasher's a violent offender. If he's mean enough to assault an old man, he wouldn't mind hurting a child."

Sarah nodded and hastened back to her vehicle.

We reached Heidi's property and parked the cruiser on the shoulder. We left, following a snow-covered trail through the brush. The small log cabin was soon in sight, a faint glow illuminating its front windows.

"If they're high, it could be a piece of cake," Heidi stated. "Hopefully, they'll only come to their senses once they're locked up in the tank."

My sister indicated a back window where we could observe the offenders discreetly. Jake Thrasher and Ken McLeod were sitting on an old sofa, their faces revealed by the flames of emergency candles arranged in a row on the coffee table. Matches and cocaine paraphernalia lay scattered around a piece of white cardboard.

"What are they doing?"

"I think they're playing a board game. Looks like a makeshift Ouija board."

The cabin was poorly lit, but we both swore we saw a black mist materialize and hover above the two men. I believe we were witnessing what is sometimes referred to as ectoplasm; the curious matter extended and swirled until it surrounded the players. Both men were absorbed in their game; they did not seem to notice the manifestation, but Thrasher suddenly sat up and looked straight in front of him. McLeod became agitated as his companion engaged in a serpent-like dance, his head leaning forward in sudden thrusts. McLeod backed away. Heidi and I feared a fight might soon erupt and thought it best to act quickly. We cocked our revolvers and opened the door. We walked in at once, our weapons pointed at the confused men: "Jake Thrasher, you are under arrest for breaking and entering, theft, physical assault and drug possession," I declared. "You do not have to say anything unless you wish to do so. You have nothing to hope from any promise of favour and nothing to fear from any threat whether or not you say anything. Anything you do or say may be used as evidence. Do you understand?"

I spoke calmly, seizing Thrasher's wrists and placing the handcuffs around them. The man was surprisingly docile and allowed me to do my business unhindered. However, McLeod was panic-stricken. He brutally pushed Heidi out of his way and made a run for it. My sister was soon on her feet, pursuing the man outside as he jumped on the stolen snowmobile and rode away into the bush. Heidi fired three shots and grazed McLeod's knee, but this did not stop the fugitive who disappeared at the end of the trail.

I pushed Thrasher to lead him out of the cabin. I believed the man to still be under the influence until his body stiffened. With one quick pull, Jake Thrasher broke the chain off his cuffs and gave a solid punch to my stomach.

"Heidi!" I cried.

My sister walked in to see Thrasher grip me by my patrol coat, lifting my body into the air and hurling me effortlessly across the room. I landed on my coccyx and my vision was immediately obscured from the shock.

"Sweet Jesus!" Heidi whispered, her hands trembling on her weapon.

Thrasher became very still. He turned around, his dilated pupils filled with black hatred, so much so that Heidi's heart skipped a beat; she had the distinctive feeling that the soul staring at her was not human and wished to shred her to pieces.

"I can't bear that name!" the man shrieked, retreating to the darkest corner of the lodge.

Thrasher's bloodcurdling voice sounded like that of a bitter old woman and presented an accent Heidi could not identify. I still laid flat on my back, my legs and spine throbbing with pain. Heidi held Thrasher at gunpoint and could only think of reciting the Lord's Prayer in her mind.

*Our Father which art in heaven, hallowed be thy name...*

"Stop it!" the man howled.

*Your kingdom come, your will be done on earth, as it is in heaven...*

"Shut up!"

*...Lead us not into temptation, but deliver us from evil: for thine is the kingdom, and the power, and the glory, for ever...*

Thrasher bounced out of the shadows, his face distorted with the most threatening expression Heidi had ever seen on a man. He ran to her, but she promptly pulled the trigger. The bullet pierced Thrasher's right arm and stopped him in his thrust. The thin man fell on Heidi who quickly crawled away from the limp body.

"...Is he dead?" I asked, after a moment.

Heidi took Thrasher's pulse.

"He's unconscious… I only winged him."

Heidi knelt down by my side.

"Jasper, are you hurt? Can you move?"

"I can. Can you help me up?"

My dizziness was slowly dissipating. Heidi pulled me to my feet and helped me sit on the sofa. She lit up the room using a fuel lantern and sat close to me, keeping a sharp eye on Thrasher.

"What on earth was that?" she mumbled, calling for an ambulance.

I inspected the cardboard game on which the alphabet had been written by hand as well as the numbers 1234567890 and the words "Yes" and "No".

"It *is* a Ouija board," I confirmed.

I examined the chunk of spruce bark the players had used as a planchette.

"You've played this game before?"

"No, but a friend of mine used to own one and often shared his eerie experiences. He got rid of it in the end."

I exposed Thrasher's wrist still enclosed in a shackle bracelet, a broken chain dangling from it.

"I daresay he was possessed."

"Possessed?" Heidi echoed. "Is he still?"

"I can't tell. Most of his symptoms can be explained by cocaine addiction, but considering his muscle mass, his phenomenal strength doesn't make any sense."

I unlocked both bracelets to keep as evidence. Heidi was afraid to touch Thrasher but agreed to fetch the first-aid kit to stop his bleeding. I removed the man's shirt and noticed deep scratch marks on his chest. We were both relieved to hear the paramedics' siren in the distance. Thrasher was taken away and was still unconscious when he was admitted to the hospital.

Heidi and I studied the tracks left by the stolen snowmobile.

"He's headed to Sarah's quarry," Heidi said.

We drove over to Roy Elias' cabin to ask if the family had seen the outlaw. Heidi knocked. Sarah Kudlak opened the door with a sigh of relief.

"Are you folks all right?" I asked.

"We're fine."

"McLeod's escaped us. He went your way. You didn't happen to see him, did you?"

"I don't know, but a snowmobile passed by real fast less than an hour ago."

Sarah let us in. Vi Elias was sewing mukluks by the stove while her husband stretched out muskrat pelts for drying. Aluki was sitting cross-legged on the floor, feeding raw muskrat meat to a husky puppy who clearly enjoyed having the girl run her toy comb through his thick fur.

"Where's Thrasher? Did you arrest him?" Sarah asked.

"He's in the hospital. I had to shoot. He attacked Jasper and would have attacked me. Have a look at this."

I opened the clear plastic bag containing our evidence and handed Thrasher's cuffs to Sarah.

"He broke his cuffs? How?"

I mimicked the convict's pulling movement with a click of the tongue.

"I swear something ungodly was going on out there," Heidi said. "I saw Thrasher lift Jasper's whole body and toss him as if he was as light as a feather. You saw the guy on the news… He's tiny. Smaller than me."

"We also found this," I added, showing her the makeshift board game.

Sarah took a step back.

"Heidi, you should burn this."

"We can't; it's evidence," I replied.

"Well, take it out of here! Dear God, it's just like the Gadarene man in the gospels."

Sergeant Matthews' voice came on my radio: "Constable Nelson?"

"Yes sir, I'm listening."

"Looks like Ken McLeod was convicted of sin, righteousness and judgment. We just found him shaking and crying like a baby at the Igloo Church."

"What about the snowmobile?"

"He'd left it by the church door. Where are you now?"

"We're still on the trapline."

"Wrap it up and return to the detachment."

We drove back to town, completed our paperwork and called it a night.

"Your boiler's been fixed, right?" Heidi asked, zipping up her patrol coat.

"The repairman is coming tomorrow."

"What? It must be the Tuktoyaktuk community freezer in there."

"Oh, some warm blankets and I'll be fine."

"Jasper, I can't let you; it's too cold. Come to my place until it's fixed. Please."

I acquiesced without fussing. Heidi secretly dreaded spending the night alone after such a disturbing scene on the trapline, but she only admitted this to me later on. She couldn't forget Thrasher's look and unnatural voice. Childhood was the last time she'd experienced this kind of fear. How disheartening to live in this continuous night with no morning to ease your anxiety! Physical danger, she had grown hardy enough to face head on, but this was immaterial; how could she comprehend or classify it?

I thought supper at the convivial Café Gallery would take our minds off things. It did for a while; hearing merry folk planning Christmas gatherings was somewhat comforting. The clash between this joie de vivre and the glance we'd been granted into the abyss was startling. And with this opposition, I believe my sister and I grasped an aspect of the holiday we had never reflected on before. We had touched the cornerstone.

We finished our meal and faced the cold, heading southeast on the Mackenzie Road. The wind was particularly cruel that night. The bright lantern glowing under the moose rack was a welcome sight when Heidi's house finally appeared at the end of the street.

"Oh man, my legs feel like icicles," Heidi declared as she took her boots off.

She undid her hair and changed her uniform shirt for a woollen sweater. I'd been fascinated to discover that beyond the strict police hairstyle, my sister's locks are rather wild and wavy. The contrast amused me.

"Are you laughing at my hair again?"

"I'm not."

"You are."

"It's like a whole new persona," I chuckled, loosening my necktie.

We sat down to watch the evening news, eager to see if the Thrasher case would be mentioned by the media.

"Can you grab that throw?" Heidi asked, indicating a fur heap by the sofa.

I reached down and unfolded the featherweight assemblage of light-coloured pelts.

"My goodness, where did you get this? It must be worth thousands of dollars."

"Nah. They're just rabbit skins I tanned and saved through the years. Vi Elias helped me sew them together. We had a good time. It's not worth much, but it's warm."

Heidi spread the throw over our legs and put an end to our shivering. Thrasher was never named, but we listened attentively for development regarding the new Nunavut government. Seeing this large piece of land separate and become a territory of its own earlier that year had inspired melancholy and curiosity all at once. Yet, the news anchor's soothing voice and physical exhaustion got the better of us, and we were soon asleep under our furry blanket.

We were halfway through the *Red Green Christmas Special* when the sound of a truck driving by roused me from slumber. My eyes instantly fell on ribbons of white light dancing across the inky skies. Aurora Borealis! I was already up and leaning against the sill, my breath condensing on the cold glass.

"Heidi, look!"

Heidi awoke to Red Green throwing a piece of fruit cake into a woodstove: "You know, fruit cake has the same properties as wood, including taste. You can keep a stove going for hours. And here's some: Use a piece of fruit cake as a lovely parking brake. Use fruit cake as a boat anchor..."

My sister frowned in confusion.

"No, the lights!" I cried, pointing to the window. "Let's go see them!"

"Jasper, it's thirty-five below with the windchill."

"It's been years since I last saw this! I'd been looking forward to it!"

I hastened to put my boots and coat on.

"Are you coming?" I insisted.

Heidi grunted and curled up on the sofa, pulling the fur throw over her head.

I ran outside, gaping in wonder as I progressed through the crisp snow; I could almost forget the glacial air running down my neck. I stopped a few steps away from the spruce barrier surrounding my sister's house. The edentulous conifers formed an asymmetrical lace above which the luminous veil flowed in smooth movements, an ever-changing picture surpassing any abstract painter's creation. Stars and distant planets offered a stable chart for these patterns to unfold against, marking the expanse in bright specks scintillating with the aurora's undulations. Love and delight pulsed hard through my chest; a powerful need to share this beauty came over me and dampened my joy until I heard the sound of Heidi's footsteps following my trail in the snow.

"Heidi, you've changed your mind?"

Heidi cast the fur throw over my shoulders.

"You must be freezing in that short patrol coat."

"What about you?"

"My parka's warm enough."

"The wind's died down."

"Yes."

I drew my sister under the throw. We huddled together and watched the parading lights until we could barely feel our faces anymore. Heidi was silent. This sort of spectacle illuminated the sky on a regular basis in the High Arctic, but it was more than a natural phenomenon to her this time. It was a sign.

"I'm terrified, Jasper," she confessed under her breath. Terror had descended upon her the moment I'd left to see the aurora. She wondered if she should get her cabin blessed by a priest. The otherworldly experience had cracked her soul open to a greater understanding of all things – material and spiritual. This strange Christmastide culminating with the new year's first sunrise would take an air of victory as the child in the manger revealed himself in his full significance.

Jake Thrasher was found dead of undetermined causes in his hospital bed the next day.

# FRAGILE VESSELS
## (CONSTABLE FINLAY)

"*IT IS IMPOSSIBLE BUT THAT OFFENCES will come: but woe unto him, through whom they come! It were better for him that a millstone were hanged about his neck, and he cast into the sea, than that he should offend one of these little ones."*

I will start with this scripture from the Gospel of Luke because it rang particularly true to me when Sergeant Nathaniel Matthews of the Inuvik detachment quoted it two months ago. I did not know where it was from, but he told me where to look when I asked about it today. I have long made fun of my sergeant behind his back for his odd religiosity, but I have come to see he often has the last laugh.

Sergeant Matthews attends the First Bible Baptist Church on Mackenzie Road. He is married and has two sons and a daughter whom I understand are named after Old Testament judges. He is a Southerner from

Saskatchewan and was transferred to our detachment three years ago. I was raised Catholic myself. We have a beautiful church here in Inuvik, which they call the Igloo Church because it looks like an igloo, but its real name is Our Lady of Victory. It is the most impressive piece of architecture in these parts. Even my brother, who has travelled much and lived in Vancouver, thinks it is a fine building. Sergeant Matthews' church is a plain clapboard house with a brown cross nailed across the side, but they have no residential school blood on their hands, and I respect them for it.

This has little to do with the events I will recall here, but I am not used to writing, except police reports. I have never been one to keep a journal, and I have no literary pretension of any kind. I was personally involved in the investigation into Nellie Isaac's disappearance last July, and this is the real subject I want to tackle here. Hopefully, the verse will make sense to you by the time you are done reading this. I say I was involved, and that is in my capacity as the sole female officer at the aforementioned detachment that currently consists of thirteen constables, a sergeant, a corporal, six civilian employees and a betta fish named Ed Buckley. There was a fourteenth constable when these events took place, but you will see why he is no longer working with us. A recent addition to our detachment is my brother Jasper Nelson whose résumé consists of six postings, including three in Nunavut where he learned to speak Inuktitut fluently.

I think it is relevant to expand on this family business, and I will tell it like it is. My brother is our father's legitimate son, and I was born out of wedlock ten years later. This has earned me the "bastard Mountie" nickname I am not very fond of. Back in 1974, my father travelled to Inuvik to hunt sheep in the Richardson Mountains in the hope of getting a Dall ram trophy for his home office. He did score a full-curl specimen that day and had a few celebratory drinks at the hotel, where he met my mother Mabel Finlay. She'd also come hunting, but for something altogether different. He bragged about his catch, they went up to his room, and I leave the rest to your imagination. I was born nine months later. My brother heard about this two years ago and set out to find me. We met in Regina last year where he handed me half the money he'd inherited from our father's estate. I had not expected to fly back to the territories with a brother and a $250,000 cheque in my pocket, but that is how it happened. Jasper had shared his part and called me his sister on his own free will. This move puzzles me to this day, and for months I thought there had to be a catch. Turns out he is a generous man, and that is all there is to it.

Jasper once said finding me has made him feel complete. Now, I can't figure out what a girl like me could add to this man's life. Jasper Nelson was raised in a well-off family. His mother, Jane Dennett, is a scholar who fed him more knowledge and theories than one could ever digest. He is handsome enough and has such a classy way with people I don't think he knows what having a foe means. I once heard a felon thanking him as he locked him up for assault. That was a first for the Inuvik detachment. The phrase "golden boy" would apply quite literally as both his hair and eyes are a golden colour. It is so peculiar that you tend to focus on this and lose track of what he is telling you. It took me a while to get used to it.

I will speak freely of my brother because I don't intend to show this to him, well-read as he is. I don't think he would ridicule me because he is a very loving man and wouldn't hurt my feelings on purpose, but I am mostly writing this to make sense of it all. The way Jasper Nelson walked into my life reminds me that God exists when I start doubting that he does. He couldn't have known I had just lost my house to my husband's gambling habit and his timely gift would help me out of the ditch. It has been a great comfort for me to have him close.

The Inuvik detachment makes for an odd assortment of officers. Some of us have been assigned here for our extensive knowledge of Inuvialuit and Gwich'in cultures and the bond of trust we have established with the locals; the rest are usually Southerners who have been transferred here for various reasons, often disciplinary ones. Inuvik's climate and social issues are challenging, and the RCMP seems to perceive our detachment as a boot camp for wayward officers. I do not like this at all, but what can you do? I have no power over it. Our corporal is an Inuvialuk named Ruben Alunik. He was raised in Inuvik and knows the place like the back of his hand. We get along right fine. He is tall and heavy, and some of his friends call him Grizzly. I never call him that because I have realized he is self-conscious about his size. I am a small blonde woman myself, and I believe people find it funny when they see us patrolling the streets together; that's how striking the contrast is. I will say this right away. I can defend myself, and I am not easily intimidated. But I feel safe when Alunik is around, and I also feel safe with my brother Jasper Nelson. It is a pleasant sensation I never knew growing up with a single mother, no matter how strong and clever she was.

I mentioned a husband. I did feel this to some extent with this man named Duncan Forrester. I lived with him for three years before he ran away and left me with all his debt. A former neighbour of ours who recently moved to British Columbia called me at the detachment last April. He had seen Duncan begging on the streets of Vancouver and asked if I was aware of this. I was not. He tried to get some explanation out of him, but Duncan ignored him, visibly ashamed of his present condition. I feel sorry for him but can't help seeing how he did this to himself. I don't know what to think. When you realize the man you once trusted has hidden significant things from you, it turns your world on its head. You think everything has been a lie, and you don't know who he is and who you are anymore.

But that is a lot of description, and I will get to the investigation proper. It happened this way. Inuvik holds its annual Great Northern Arts Festival in July. It is a time when the Arctic experiences a phenomenon they call the "midnight sun". This whole thing draws many visitors and artisans from all over the place – even people from outside Canada. This means extra work and patrolling for us RCMP officers to make sure everybody is safe and parties are kept under control. One day, Jasper and I were on our patrol route and we stopped by the community greenhouse to see the gardens and talk with people. That is part of building the trust. If there is anything I look at with pride in this town, it is the community greenhouse. I am no gardener myself, but the symbolic aspect of the place is close to my heart. It was built last year, when they got rid of the Grollier Hall arena and used the structure for a public garden space.

Grollier Hall and Stringer Hall were two Church-run residential schools that the government made Aboriginal children attend in the sixties. You cannot imagine the kind of abuse that went on there. The schools were eventually closed and this arena converted. Seeing lush vegetation replace the painful memories is part of the healing process for many. Anyhow, Jasper and I were talking to my childhood friend, Sarah Kudlak, who had a small plot of her own, when I noticed a long-haired man looking at us from across the arena. He was listening to my brother cite a list of plant names and smiling to himself.

"Jasper, that man's been staring at you for a while," I said. "Do you know him?"

Jasper looked up.

"Good heavens, Jay Isaac! That's the man who shot that wood bison and saved my life when I was posted in Carmacks."

"Your friend from the Yukon?"

Jasper nodded and walked up to him.

Jasper's first posting was at the Carmacks detachment. While on duty there, he was sent to investigate a fatal car accident near Little Salmon First Nation. A mean bison suddenly emerged from the bush and charged. Jasper's training had not prepared him for this sort of occurrence; he'd spent his whole existence in cities and encountering wildlife makes him uneasy to this day. Fortunately, a Northern Tutchone trapper happened to drive by and witness the scene.

"Get down!" he cried, and Jasper swiftly crawled under his cruiser. Jay Isaac pulled his rifle and discharged four .338 Winchester Magnum rounds into the bull's chest. Jasper was unharmed, and I am deeply grateful to Isaac for his kindness and quick thinking.

"Last I heard of you, you'd been sent to the North Pole," the man said, shaking my brother's hand.

"You mean Grise Fiord? That was a while ago. I spent some time in Vancouver, and my superior had me transferred here in September. Are you here for the festival?"

"I am. My wife Nellie's paintings are exhibited at the complex."

"Are they, now? We were there just an hour ago. What paintings are these?"

"Animals and people mostly. Traditional stuff. She's right by the door, wearing a burnt orange shirt."

"I remember her," I said. "You talked to her, Jasper."

My brother introduced me and tried to sum up our singular family history. Jay Isaac listened and nodded.

"Jasper told me he could have died had you not intervened that day," I said. "I feel indebted to you."

"I wish you'd had a taste of that bison meat," he replied. "…I'd heard of what you'd done with this place. I wanted to see it for myself."

"It certainly warms the heart," Jasper said.

I said nothing because it got me thinking about Grollier Hall, and I felt ashamed to be a white woman.

We headed back to the Midnight Sun Complex as soon as our shift ended. Jasper wanted to buy some art to hang on his wall and purchased a salmon painting from Nellie Isaac. The fish was drawn in a Tlingit style with many intricate details. The picture's background was entirely black and the salmon entirely red.

"That is fitting for a Mountie," Nellie giggled.

I will mention Nellie Isaac is one of the most beautiful women I have ever seen. It is sadly one of the reasons why what happened to her happened. There was something very warm about her that made you feel like she was an old friend, even if you had just met her.

The wind was strong enough to control the mosquito flow that night, so my brother and I put some insect repellent on and went out for a walk. The sky was full of colourful clouds as the sun entered its false setting phase from which to rise yet again. Something must be said about my brother's gait at this point. Jasper Nelson walks with his toes upwards, making broad shoulder swings to the sides like a sort of dance. It is a funny sight, yet he walks with assurance and does not seem to perceive how odd this is. I can't help smiling about it at times. If Jasper Nelson had not sought me out and spoken to me first last year, making his acquaintance would not have crossed my mind, as you can spot the golden boy aura a mile away. He belongs to a class of people I usually have no business meddling with, but this unique manner of walking helped me see his earthly dimension.

Jasper is generally well liked, and he doesn't have to try. He had only been in Inuvik for a few months when I started noticing women flocking around him (men as well, but in a different way), and the picture was not unlike that of the popular kid in the schoolyard. Drinking makes my brother social, and he will cheer and join in the game while I stand at the back like an outsider looking in. I feared he would soon forget I had anything to do with his transfer to Inuvik, make new friends and avoid taking his bastard sister with him the way you would not hang a gold pendant on a piece of twine. It did not happen, though. Jasper's work and responsibilities are his priority, and socializing is something he only engages in when the opportunity arises. He is so engrossed in filing his domestic violence report the next day that he barely remembers the girl hitting on him the night before. I will say his notion of human ties is hard to grasp and let it go at that.

We passed by Jay Isaac's camper on our way. The man was sitting by himself, roasting sausages over an open fire. A russet Malamute dog came out from under the bushes and started barking at us.

"Kw'anintsi!" Jay chided.

The dog ran up to us to investigate the potential intruders.

"I'm sorry."

"Don't be," Jasper replied, running his hand though the canine's thick coat.

"Is your wife here with you?" I asked.

"She was invited to a party near Campbell Lake. She asked me to go, but I don't like crowds. I told her to enjoy herself and come back early."

"Are we a crowd?" I hesitated.

Jay grinned. He got up, unfolded two camping chairs and invited us to join him.

"You want some?" Jay said, handing the sausage pack over.

"We just had supper. Thank you very much, though," Jasper answered.

"Did you make them yourself?" I asked.

"I did. It's bear meat. We had them in the freezer, and I'd forgotten about them."

"Do you hunt and trap for a living?"

Jay nodded.

"Any improvement on the water contamination issues in Little Salmon?" Jasper asked.

"Nope. Nellie and I got a bellyful of it and moved to Carmacks a few years ago. It was a non-stop boil water advisory. That's when we decided to get married, and she moved in with me. She's been trying to raise awareness with that art of hers."

"Art can be a powerful instrument," Jasper replied. "It moves hearts and minds and pushes its message in a mysterious way. In the late eighteenth century, a British artisan named Josiah Wedgwood created a white jasper medallion featuring the black basalt relief figure of an African slave in chains. The words 'Am I not a slave and a brother?' surrounded the figure to underline the humanity of the black slaves and denounce the unjust treatment they were subjected to. Four years later, thousands of these medallions had been distributed and had a significant influence on the public's opinion of slavery."

"The wells were originally dug by the federal government decades ago," Jay explained. "Because of poor planning, they were built below ground level which caused for ground water runoff and contamination. The government knows all about it but refuses to fund repairs. I guess something like the Walkerton outbreak will have to happen before they decide to budge."

"Don't lose heart, Jay. Things can get better, even when it looks rotten to the bone. In Wedgwood's days, slavery was a major pillar in the economy, child labour was rampant and animal cruelty was widely accepted. When humanity reaches a low, we might be tempted to think this is the end and things can never get better. Yet, social reforms brought by handfuls of righteous men changed the course of history, and we look back in awe at how this wickedness was tolerated at all. I'm confident that if we persevere, the government's attitude *will* change."

"If you say so," Jay Isaac replied, with much scepticism.

Jane Dennett's bookcase had sure filled my brother's head with all sorts of romantic ideas. I hear she fed her son H.G. Wells novels growing up and that had a lasting influence on his understanding of society. She'd made up her mind to turn him into a politician; dirt road policing was not her first career choice for him. She had hoped he'd earn a university degree and improve needy people's lives with studies and statistics instead of handling the sludge for himself. Jasper says witnessing human suffering first-hand adjusted the faulty perspectives he once held on life. I believe it did, but he could use some more grounding if you ask me. Don't get me wrong. I admire Jasper's determination to attain the greater good, but his trust in government institutions makes him naïve at times. Ideas and reality get muddled in his head.

I prefer to be on my guard. My impression is that this Liberal government will tell you whatever you want to hear but then do what suits it best or nothing at all in the end. It is a big mask show, and I do not fall for masquerades. The reason the Canadian people keep electing those spendthrift actors is one of life's mysteries. When I think about how Southerners are making decisions for us up North when they haven't got the slightest idea of what is going on, my blood boils. Still, it's strangely uplifting to listen to someone like Jasper Nelson when you think everything is going down the drain. People like him exist for a reason.

The wind was blowing smoke in my face, and I moved my chair to the right. I soon discovered Jay Isaac was a man of few words. He paid close attention and his perceptive eyes displayed great intelligence, but he only graced you with a few sharp replies to keep the conversation going. Jasper did most of the talking. He ended up feeling bad about it, so he tried to get us involved. It did not work out as he wished. It was getting late, and I really wanted to use the short-lived twilight to help me get to sleep before the sun started shining its bright polar day face at us at four in the morning. We said goodbye and headed back home.

We met some children running outside on the way. You can't blame them for being up so late with the sun playing tricks on their sense of time.

"It's past eleven, kids," I said.

They all froze and stared quietly. A shy girl ran straight home, and Jasper chuckled.

"You sure know how to inspire fear of authority," he whispered. "They recognize you, even without the uniform."

I am not certain the children's fear solely came from their associating me with the RCMP or my five-year-old goddaughter, Aluki Kudlak, repeatedly threatening the neighbourhood's naughty kids to call me so I could "put the cuffs on them."

I found over twenty mosquitoes waiting for me in my room that night. Those nasty suckers will find their way in, even when you are careful to keep your doors and windows shut at all times. I went on a killing spree, and it was past midnight when I finally managed to get some sleep.

I did not expect to see much of Jay or Nellie Isaac after that. But Jay showed up at the detachment a quarter after ten the following morning. I greeted him with a smile and soon noticed his long face and tired eyes.

"Hi Jay. What brings you here?" I asked.

"...Nellie never came back from the party last night."

"What?"

"I asked everyone at the complex and nobody's seen her. The girl who gave her a ride to Campbell Lake said she looked for her at the end of the night and didn't find her. She assumed she'd left with someone else and went on home."

Jasper and Alunik joined us and had Jay file a missing person report. They tried to reassure him, saying his wife had possibly had too much to drink and whoever had given her a ride had also offered her a warm bed to sleep in. We opened an investigation and promised to keep in touch. One of the festival's photographers had taken a few good shots of Nellie, and we used one of his pictures for our posters. Considering Nellie's orange shirt, we were pretty sure she would soon be found if she was still wearing such conspicuous clothing. Jay was relieved and left to continue his search. It was almost noon when two young women arrived at the detachment with a disturbing lead that screamed out foul play. They were local drum dancers who had struck up a friendship with Nellie during the festival.

"We saw something we think you should know about," the eldest girl said. "Nellie was speaking to a guy named Rudy Ayak last night, and he started harassing her. She tried to shoo him off and walked away, but he kept following her around. He kissed her and pulled her arm. I saw them head towards the bush. That's the last I saw of Nellie last night."

"Were there any drugs or alcohol involved?" Jasper asked.

"Rudy was drunk. He couldn't think straight. And he's a hard one to read; you never know what's in his head, you see? Nellie had had a few beers for sure. I don't think she was all there either."

"Does Rudy live here in Inuvik?"

"Yes, he was in my class," the youngest girl said. "He works at the grocery store."

"Was Rudy seen at the party later?"

"I saw him passed out on a camping chair, yes."

The possibility of Nellie Isaac being lost in the bush or lying cold and lifeless in a ditch imposed itself at once. Corporal Alunik organized a search party and Jay joined us on our way to Campbell Lake, some twenty kilometres southeast of Inuvik. He had brought a piece of his wife's clothing for Kw'anintsi to sniff and put his snout to good use. Jasper, our colleague Don Clark and I were part of the team, along with fourteen volunteers who knew the campground well. Constable Clark brought two men with him in the patrol vessel to cruise the waters. The campground is far enough from the lake, but you never know what is in a drunken person's mind, and a drunken person running away from an assailant at that. The rest of us explored the surrounding wilderness with Kw'anintsi giving it all he'd got. That dog meant business.

Jay kept quiet, but you could read the distress in his face. He called out his wife's name from time to time and would choke up every time. As a hunter, I knew Jay should have been attentive to unusual tracks or broken branches, but he was in a haze and simply followed, relying on the search and rescue team to notice these things for him. Jasper Nelson's attention to detail is razor-sharp, and I knew he would not let anything slip by. He once got a Vancouver Triad leader arrested for MDMA manufacturing by noting a faint licorice smell in a neighbourhood he'd often drive through on his patrol route.

We had been searching the woods for twenty minutes when Corporal Alunik called me on my radio: "Constable Finlay?"

"Yes?"

"Are you with the search party?"

"I am. Nothing so far. We're in the bush, and I sure hope Nellie Isaac isn't. Bugs would have carried her away by now. Black flies are having a party of their own down here."

"We got this Rudy Ayak in custody... Lacasse is trying to bully a story out of him, and I don't like his methods. I want a second opinion."

"All right, I'm on my way."

I ran back to the campground and drove into town. You might be wondering why Corporal Alunik needed my input in particular, and the story goes as follows. When I joined the Inuvik detachment in 1995, Alunik noticed my uncanny ability to tell when suspects and witnesses were hiding some key information from us. During an investigation into a major bootlegging operation in 1997, I was the only officer who managed to see through our suspect's scheme after throwing some questions at him. The alcohol had been concealed in laundry detergent containers, and we intercepted the shipment before it made its way to Fort McPherson that day. Alunik has entrusted me with tricky suspects ever since.

I joined Alunik behind the one-way mirror and listened to Lacasse intimidate Rudy Ayak as you would a rotten piece of fish: "You don't remember? I'm not a fool. I see exactly what 'appened. You were so drunk and so 'igh you raped that girl, you killed her and you went to 'ide her in a shallow grave. And you don't even remember it."

"I didn't hurt her, I swear!" Ayak cried.

"You went back to the party *ni vu ni connu,* and you thought we wouldn't find out?"

Ayak was on the verge of tears. He had no criminal record, and Lacasse's insistence was inappropriate at best. Now, Constable Lacasse is one of those officers who had been transferred to the Inuvik detachment for misconduct. I did not know the particulars at the time. One thing we had all discovered, though, is that he hated Aboriginal people to a high degree. Having Alunik as his superior was a big blow for him. He was originally from Val-d'Or, Quebec and spoke broken English which did not help establish his credibility in the community.

Alunik ordered Lacasse to leave and introduced me to our suspect. Rudy Ayak was an Inuvialuk in his early twenties. I didn't know what his attitude was like when they'd arrested him, but Lacasse had broken him by then, and I wondered if this would help us or not. I had the strange impression I was playing good cop in the good cop/bad cop dynamic. It is usually the other way around with my brother, who is more compassionate than I am. I have come to see that Jasper Nelson's passion for justice stems from his desire to defend the little guy, while getting the bad guy is more my thing. I sat across the table from Ayak, and here is what I read in his face: *There is no justice here.* I refused to let him get away with that belief.

"Don't worry, Rudy, I won't try to make you admit to a crime you didn't commit. Can I call you Rudy?"

He nodded but hesitated to look me in the eye. This could be a sign that someone is lying, but in this case, I knew it was confusion. He was humiliated and had given up hope of being treated fairly. He eventually grew comfortable enough to look up, and I believe he recognized me. He was only a few years younger than me, and we had often seen each other in school growing up.

"I just want to get the facts straight."

"I didn't lie to that man."

"I don't think you're a liar. But you're the last person who spoke to Nellie Isaac before she went missing, and you probably have information we badly need."

"I wouldn't want anything bad to have happened to her because of me."

"Did something bad happen?"

"I don't know!"

"I know you were drunk, and it might be a blur, but could you describe your interaction with Nellie Isaac to the best of your ability? What was it like?"

"She was really nice to me at first… She saw me sitting there by myself. She smiled and came to talk to me. I suppose she felt sorry for me. I was drunk, and I wanted to think she meant it."

"Romantically, you mean?"

Rudy Ayak blushed.

"Did she tell you she was married?"

"She did later."

"What did you talk about? Did she have any intentions of going somewhere else?"

"I don't think she did. She told me about her artwork and her home in the Yukon. She asked what my plans were. I didn't have much to say about that."

"We have two witnesses who saw you follow her around and hold her back when she tried to get away from you. What happened there?"

Ayak looked down.

"I was drunk; I didn't mean to hurt her."

"Our witnesses saw you kiss her."

"She told me she was married then. I insisted, and she got angry. She walked away and yelled at me. I followed her for a while and then returned to the campground. I drank some more, and I don't remember anything after that."

"She was not seen again. Did she head deeper into the bush?"

"Seems to me she was heading for the highway."

That affirmation could only be the clean truth or a dirty lie. I kept silent for an entire minute. Ayak was puzzled at this, but nothing indicated he was lying. All I could see was a miserable man ashamed of his drunken behaviour. There was a lot of fear in his eyes, and the way I understood it, he hadn't known until then that something like this could get him into such trouble. I also think he felt genuine remorse for the impact his actions might have had on Nellie Isaac's present situation.

I left the interrogation room. Lacasse and Alunik awaited me behind the glass.

"I don't believe he hurt her," I said. "He did harass her and admitted to it, but he let her go when she told him to get lost. She might have wandered into the bush, trying to get away from him. Or she might have decided to hitch-hike her way back to town, only to fall in the hands of a true predator."

Lacasse turned pale when I suggested this.

"It might not be foul play after all," Alunik replied.

"You really believe this crap?" Lacasse snapped.

"Shut up, Lacasse… I suppose the possibility of an attack by a wild animal is also worth considering."

While I was away at the detachment, Kw'anintsi picked up a trail and led Jasper to the Dempster Highway. They were a fifteen minutes' walk from the campground, when my brother spotted a tiny blue bead in the gravel.

"Did you find something?" Jay asked.

"Does this look familiar to you?"

Jay examined the object.

"There was some beadwork on Nellie's skirt… I suppose some of the stitches might have come undone as she walked through the brush."

They kept looking and found a few more along the shoulder.

"She came all this way," Jasper said. "If someone offered her a ride and didn't bring her back to you, she could be anywhere at this point."

Jasper told me he immediately felt he shouldn't have spoken his mind because it made the situation look hopeless and laid a heavier load on Jay, who was already weighed down. Alunik informed the search party about Rudy Ayak's testimony. The party explored Campbell Lake until the end of Clark and Jasper's shift. Kw'anintsi was tired and could not smell much of anything anymore. Alunik suggested they get back to town until a new lead showed us where to look. We had to rely on the local population to spot Nellie and call us at this point. I was at the detachment when Jasper returned. He waved a little plastic bag at me.

"You got those beads in there?"

Jasper let me have a look at them.

"How far from the campground?"

"About a kilometre."

"Sure seems to confirm Rudy Ayak's impression… Where's Jay?"

"He went back to his camper. He's exhausted in every possible way. He barely slept last night."

Lacasse came up behind us, asking to see the evidence for himself.

"And what is this supposed to be?"

"Beads," Jasper answered. "The kind used by Northern Tutchone women in their traditional beadwork. This was part of a flower pattern sewn on Nellie Isaac's skirt."

Lacasse snickered.

"You're not serious. There's so many freaking Indians in town these days! What makes you think this is hers?"

Jasper and I frowned, knowing he would have never dared to talk in this fashion in front of Ruben Alunik. We'd had to insist on Lacasse using the word "freaking" instead of another similar-sounding word because of how offensive it is to our culture. He did not understand it at first. He said it is commonly used in Quebec and no one bats an eye.

"Her husband recognized them," Jasper said.

"How can you recognize a thing like that?"

"Do you have a problem, Lacasse? You're not being helpful," I snapped.

I was truly irritated to see this incompetent sneer at my brother's discovery; he made Jasper's stunning sense of observation look silly.

"Yes, I have a problem. My problem is that you let that suspect go."

Lacasse had been a ball and chain to all of us since his arrival in Inuvik, but his attitude was plain irrational in this case. I think he disliked the way I stared and tried to read his intentions because he walked away right there.

"I can't stand him," I muttered.

Jasper kept his mouth shut. He can show remarkable self-control when it comes to impatience. Which doesn't mean you can't detect it in his face. We left the detachment and saw Lacasse at the wheel of one of our patrol cars, looking around as if he'd lost something he desperately needed to find in there.

I went home but could not get much rest knowing Nellie Isaac was either battling it out with black bears and insect swarms or sequestrated by an abductor we had no information about. It is one thing to fight crime all day and punch out when you know the victims are safe, but quite another when there is a missing person in pain out there. Some say you must learn to disconnect. I can't. Some have thrown the phrase "task-oriented" at me. They did not mean it as a compliment. But no, I felt a personal connection to Jay Isaac; it wasn't about a task or even my sense of duty. I owed him something for the good he had done to my brother. What anguish he must be feeling if I felt bad myself! I called my friend Sarah, who is very religious, and asked her to pray for Jay and Nellie Isaac. She said she already was. As for Sergeant Matthews, he once told me he prays for every single one of his constables and for the cases we are working on. Sometimes things get bad, and he takes it down to his clapboard church on Wednesday nights where there are prayers going up as if our lives depended on it. I have come to consider them my back-up team. Weird things happen when they get on their knees like that. In a good way.

THE SEARCH PARTY gathered once more the next day, and we picked up where we'd left off. It is heartening to see a community invest so much effort and compassion into rescuing a single individual, even someone they don't know very well. Alunik called Nellie Isaac's family to ask if she had tried to contact them. She had not. Had she been in touch with any shady friend or acquaintance in recent weeks? There were none they could think of. Jay neither. Nellie's relatives were worried sick and planning to come to Inuvik to join the search party. Jay was encouraged to hear our air detachment would be flying over the area first thing in the morning. I was glad to see his face light up. My belief was that Nellie had been abducted, but no one wants to be a killjoy. We were increasingly concerned, as the first forty-eight hours, which are crucial in a missing person case, were closing in on us, and we had no new lead to show us the way.

I was off duty the following day and awoke to the news that two hikers had found Nellie Isaac with a broken ankle, just a few kilometres away from my house. She was badly dehydrated and covered in insect bites. She was alive but barely. Emergency services rushed her to the hospital and saw to her needs. We were all profoundly relieved to hear she would make it and had not been attacked by a wild animal. We were also eager to hear what had happened from the horse's mouth and hoped she would soon regain consciousness.

The day was sunny and dry. I grabbed my bug jacket and went strawberry picking. I had brought two small buckets and filled them to the brim. I discovered that spot last year. It is a mighty good spot, but mosquitoes will be after you like a hungry wolverine. I could hear them tapping against the hood as loud as raindrops on a window pane. When I headed back home, old Ruth Tingmiak saw me walk by and waved at me. She is eighty-four but perfectly lucid. She was sitting on her porch, soaking up the sun.

"What have you got there, Heidi?" she asked.

"Wild strawberries."

"Lucky you! I wish I could still go berry picking, but my joints are too stiff to kneel."

"Help yourself," I said, offering her some.

We ate a few handfuls and Ruth got me talking about Nellie Isaac's ordeal.

"I hear they found that girl with the orange shirt. Do you know how she's doing?"

"She's going to be fine, Ruthie, don't worry. They're taking good care of her at the hospital and her husband is right there by her side."

"Are you going to arrest her?" she asked.

I was befuddled, to say the least.

"Arrest her? She's no criminal, Ruth, she's a victim. She went missing. She didn't do anything wrong."

"No? Why was one of you Mounties chasing after her that night? I saw him follow her into the bush. I thought he was trying to arrest her."

"Are you sure that was Nellie Isaac, Ruth?"

"My eyesight isn't all it used to be, but I can tell an orange shirt when I see one."

"Ruth, if you saw something that night, you need to come forward about it."

"Well, I heard screaming. It woke me up, and I looked out the window. That girl jumped out of one of your police cars and ran away. That Mountie was after her, and I don't know what happened next. I figured she'd escaped him when I heard she'd gone missing."

"I didn't hear about any of this. Which officer was that?"

"It was one of those Southerners. I think it was the French guy."

"Constable Lacasse? He was on patrol that night."

"I don't know his name."

I drove into town and parked by my brother's house on Breynat. His shift had just ended, and he was sitting on a chair looking at Nellie Isaac's painting on the wall.

"Jasper, I need to talk to you," I said.

He sat up, all ears because he's usually the one doing the talking and pestering me to tell him what I'm thinking even when I have nothing particular to say.

"There's a new witness in Nellie Isaac's case. I spoke to her this afternoon. Remember Ruth Tingmiak who lives southeast of town with her son and daughter-in-law?"

"Yes."

"Ruth saw what happened to Nellie from her bedroom window that night. She heard a woman screaming and saw her step out of a cruiser. She recognized Nellie's orange shirt and said she was running away into the bush with a Mountie on her heels. That Mountie could only be Lacasse."

"Lacasse?"

"I told you he'd been acting strange lately. I'm sure he was looking for lost beads in the car that day. He wanted to suppress evidence. The way I understand it, Nellie was walking away from the party and heading to town after Ayak harassed her. Lacasse saw her and offered her a ride; she trusted him because he was a policeman. He tried to force himself onto her; she ran away, hurt her ankle and got stuck in the bush."

"Heidi, that's a serious accusation you're making."

"...There's more. One night, I was on the evening shift with Lacasse, and we were alone in the bullpen. He forcibly kissed me on the neck and touched me on my private parts. He would have gone farther if I hadn't stopped him."

"What?"

"I gave him a good punch; I knocked the wind right out of him. He understood what I was about and left me alone after that."

"Heidi, why didn't you tell me about this?"

"It happened before you moved to Inuvik."

"Was he disciplined for it?"

"I didn't report it. After Duncan left and I lost the house, my work performance suffered. I was reprimanded a few times. My credibility was at an all-time low. I didn't want to lose my job. I didn't think it would escalate to this."

"He took advantage of you, and you just let him?"

"You honestly think reporting it would have made a difference? Or done any good at all? You know how common this is… Women are not taken seriously in the Force. We have to earn our spurs. And even then. This could have easily ruined my career and labelled me as a complainer. Lacasse would have gotten away with it; he would have been transferred again and pursued his dirty business elsewhere. That's how they handle these things."

"Has this happened to you before?"

"Let's say Lacasse was much bolder than the others."

Jasper was pale with wrath. You would think people get red in the face when they're angry, but no, he was white – white and indignant. I didn't know what was happening to him. I didn't know if this was about Nellie Isaac, about me or because his ideals had been shaken, but he got up and headed straight for the door.

"Jasper, don't do anything stupid," I said.

I never thought I would have to say this to my brother because he is usually calm and level-headed, but that's how changed he was.

I followed him outside. Jasper's house is only a few minutes' walk from the detachment. As we walked in, we found Jay Isaac engaged in a discussion with Sergeant Matthews and Corporal Alunik. His wife was well enough to talk and had told him about the assault. You can see how volatile the situation was.

"He offered her a hundred dollars to do it and tried to rape her when she refused! He pursued her, and God knows what he would have done to her if she hadn't run and hid from him."

"Did she describe the officer?"

"She said he had a French accent."

Lacasse was on the phone in the bullpen and did not see it coming. As soon as he hung up, Jasper grabbed him and pinned him against the wall with an arm under his jaw.

"It's all over; we have a witness, Lacasse. And I know what you did to my sister, you creep."

"What did he do to her?" Alunik asked.

"Same thing he did to Nellie Isaac. Only, Heidi fought back."

Alunik turned to me.

"When did this happen, Finlay?"

"Last year in July."

"And you didn't tell us?"

I suddenly became the centre of attention and wished I could disappear.

"Is this the kind of mentality you cultivate in this detachment, Sergeant?" Jasper said. "If a female officer gets assaulted, she's better off keeping quiet about it?"

"Certainly not!"

I thought Sergeant Matthews and Alunik would try to intervene and tell my brother to let go, but they were both astounded. Constable Lacasse's face was ashen. Perhaps he'd been under the impression he would get another transfer and manage to leave this "Indian town" he hated so much. He now had to acknowledge his defeat. He did not struggle one bit but looked terrified when Alunik came forward and bent down to look him in the eye.

"You knew where to look all this time, Lacasse? You would have been relieved to hear she was dead, wouldn't you?"

Ruben Alunik could pulverize a man with a fist if he wanted to, but he knows how to refrain himself. He took a pair of handcuffs from his belt and recited the arrest caution.

"'Be sure your sin will find you out,'" Sergeant Matthews quoted as Alunik led Lacasse to the cell block.

It's hard to tell what was in Sergeant Matthews' mind at this point. My impression is that he was sad, irritated and embarrassed for the RCMP all at once. He took me aside and said:

"Constable Finlay, did I ever give you the impression you should keep something like this to yourself?"

"No, not you in particular."

"Then who?"

"Our previous Staff Sergeant. The culture. Trying to keep up appearances. I felt it would make matters worse for me."

"I don't care for appearances, Finlay. I care about the truth. Lacasse had been transferred here for sexual misconduct. One more stain on his record, and he would have been removed from duty. Had you reported it, we could have prevented what happened to Nellie Isaac."

Did you ever feel like your interlocutor's tone is compassionate and accusatory at once? It's terribly confusing, but you always feel bad in the end.

I hung my head and cried myself silly. I think Jasper felt sorry for me, as you would for an abuse victim, like he wanted to protect me, you know? He was holding me tight and didn't understand it at all. I did not feel sorry for myself. I cried out of anger and despair. That fool Lacasse had broken everything we had worked so hard to build, had taken away the little trust we'd managed to instil in the community. Jay Isaac had gotten a double dose of federal negligence with those faulty wells in the Yukon and with a perverse RCMP officer who'd nearly gotten his wife killed. I felt very low and was ashamed to look at him. I assume he was disgusted and hoping he would never have to deal with us again.

Sergeant Matthews sent us home and told my brother to look after me. I'm not sure what he meant by that exactly. We walked back to Jasper's house, and he asked if I wanted to go home or have supper with him and talk. This whole thing weighed so heavily on me that it made me dizzy. I did not want to deal with it on my own. Jasper made sandwiches, and we had a light meal. I was not hungry at all but forced it down anyway. Sometimes, your body needs fuel, and you can think more clearly afterwards. We did not talk much at first. I didn't know what to say, but he respected it and kept quiet too. My conscience was on fire, and I needed to set things straight.

"What are you thinking about?" Jasper asked, after he'd poured us some tea.

"...Is it my fault?" I mumbled.

"What is?"

"What happened to Nellie Isaac... I didn't report what Lacasse did to me. I neglected my duty. I wasn't thinking of what he might do to others."

"Heidi, Lacasse knows the law. He had no business assaulting anyone. You can't blame yourself for this."

"Sergeant Matthews does."

"He's not one to rub salt into the wound. That's not what he meant... Why did you keep this to yourself? With all the trouble Lacasse caused, you never mentioned this to me."

"I didn't feel comfortable talking about it... Anyhow, I doubted anyone would dare to do anything like that with you around. But it's all about to hit the fan. This will be on the news. We'll have to build people's trust from scratch all over again. Sometimes, I think I should retreat to the bush, go trapping and get away from this mess. It's a sinking ship."

"Heidi, you can't do this. You're one of the few officers who really know what they're doing in this town. You understand the people; you understand their needs. They know who they can trust. They won't just throw the baby away with the bathwater."

"I'm not so sure. Trust is a fragile thing."

There are moments when life looks bleak, and this was one of them for me. I felt lonely. You could say my brother was right in front of me, and I was not alone. Well, there was something looming over me that had been pushing me down a mosquito-infested swamp of dark gloom at times. I badly needed to tell Jasper about it. I needed to know what his thinking on the matter was. You see, the prospect of either of us getting transferred to a new detachment leaves me crestfallen. The RCMP could decide to send me to Vancouver and Jasper to Newfoundland. We have little control over this sort of thing. You may ask why I became a constable in the first place if this is part of the job. I suppose I was young and foolish and only had my standing to think about at the time. I had been trying to keep my brother and my feelings at arm's length ever since it hit me like a ton of bricks. Attempting to put this into words made me tear up again.

"Heidi, what is it?"

"Jasper, I can't bear to think that sooner or later, one of us will get transferred and we'll be apart."

I cried some more and my brother cried too. I could tell it was a different feeling he had than me, though.

"I didn't know you cared that much," he said. "I wouldn't just leave, Heidi."

"There's nothing we can do about it."

He said there was. He said we would think of something. And if things got real bad, we could get into that trapping business together. I cannot imagine Jasper Nelson skinning muskrats for a living, but I knew he meant well, and I said it would suit me just fine.

Sergeant Matthews called me to his office a few days later and stressed how harassment would not be tolerated in his detachment. If anything like what Lacasse had done should happen again, I was to report it at once. I said I still felt uneasy about how higher authorities would handle the issue, but I appreciated his integrity. He answered he could not give the enemies of the Lord an occasion to blaspheme, whatever that means.

If you are under the impression I was to blame for Nellie Isaac's hardship, I will only say this in my defence: Pressing charges and dealing with a trial would have been too heavy for me to bear at the time. Sometimes, you know you have reached your breaking point, and all you can do is say: "I don't need this right now," and ignore it. I was still reeling from Duncan's stunt, losing the house and getting confirmation that my father had ignored me his whole life. I think my brother saw right through me when he said Lacasse had taken advantage of me. Predators always seek the weaker prey. It consoles me to remember his words when I feel guilty about this.

It did torment me for a while, though. Jasper had kept Nellie Isaac's business card, and I found the courage to write and apologize to her. She was puzzled. She did not want me to feel guilty and told me Jay was feeling guilty himself for failing to protect her. It was all very odd, but it made me feel better somehow. But who should be watching out to protect their wives from the police? That's how broken the RCMP is.

WE HAD OUR first snowfall today. It is three degrees below outside, and the view from my kitchen window is back to its usual self of white, blue and grey.

It has been a full year since Jasper Nelson moved here to Inuvik. I have given the Force another chance. Jasper is as optimistic as ever. He says good seeds bear good fruit, and we must keep planting. He believes good men must hold on even if all they get is scorn at first; otherwise, we'd soon be swallowed up by corruption. I don't know if I am a good man, or woman, for that matter. I certainly don't have the kind of energy and perseverance my brother seems to have in the face of adversity, although I think I once did. I sometimes wonder if Jasper's thinking is sound at all and if there really is a possibility for progress ahead.

I asked Sergeant Matthews about it once. He doesn't hold much hope for change himself because man is what he is, a sinner, he says, and "there is no new thing under the sun." His eyes are fixed on what he calls the recompense of reward which has something to do with God making all things new in the end. But he says we must still be good stewards of what has been entrusted to us and that we do get to reap benefits in this life. There *are* years of grace, he says.

# THE NAUJAAT DIARIES
## (CONSTABLE NELSON)

MARCH 6, 2005

The sky is remarkably clear tonight. I can see Ursa Major from my living room window. This reminds me of a proverb my Grise Fiord partner Sam Kunuk used to quote when faced with an insurmountable trial: "Even the strongest eagle cannot soar higher than the stars."

Today marks the sixth anniversary of my father's passing. I flipped through some of the books he bought me when I was a child, and waves of memories came crashing in with each spine. The most vivid remains the evening he read to me from Farley Mowat's *Lost in the Barrens* as I lay bedridden with bronchitis. The riveting story kept my mind off the painful cough, and I look back to these moments with great fondness and no memory of discomfort whatsoever. With all his failings, my father was an affectionate man and a lover of the arts with an open mind to the world. From him, I gained an appreciation for diplomacy and refinement, but also a sense of adventure, and I am grateful to him for it.

Life has been unusually quiet around here since Heidi left to attend her mother's funeral in Thunder Bay. Mabel Finlay succumbed to her incapacitating illness after all these years. I hear things went smoothly enough. My sister should return tomorrow. It is on nights such as these that I feel the weight of the years and wonder what life would be like if I had made different choices. Did I make the right ones? This question tends to bring traumatic images from the past, especially cases where I failed as a police officer. I try to remind myself that my work is essential, and I have saved many lives still. I wish I could erase the most horrid investigations I've had to handle from my memory, but they remain and trouble me when I least expect it.

MARCH 7, 2005

I had an enriching conversation with Constable Harris this morning. Harris is a young officer from Toronto who was transferred to the Inuvik detachment five months ago. He started off with great enthusiasm, expecting to bring significant change to the town's west side where poverty and substance abuse are an issue. He thought he could create a solid bond of trust with the residents and help improve their conditions, but has so far failed to do so. Being confronted by violent and uncooperative individuals at the drunk tank Saturday night has left him dejected, and he opened up to me about it. Constable Harris is rather alarmed to see his compassion and faith in humanity dwindle away. He has begun reading a self-help book titled

*Revive your Inner Goodness.* Heidi and Sergeant Matthews had a good laugh when they saw it on his desk, and I can't for the life of me figure out why.


M A R C H   8 ,   2 0 0 5

Sergeant Matthews called Heidi and I into his office today. He announced there is an immediate opening at the two-person detachment of Repulse Bay, V Division. Our understanding of the Inuit people and its historical trauma would be welcome in a community where an unusual number of suicides have taken place in recent months. My knowledge of Inuktitut and experience in such communities would be a major asset, he said, and since my sister and I have previously expressed our willingness to be assigned to isolated postings, he wanted to let us know about it. He prefers to see Northerners with a heart for the Inuit exercise their duties "not grudgingly, or of necessity: for God loveth a cheerful giver" rather than having young Southerners provide inept service to the needy hamlet.

I was puzzled to see Heidi nod and show a marked interest in the prospect. I expected her to hesitate since she's spent her whole existence in Inuvik and has grown deep roots in this town. There is also a chance we would not be sent back to Inuvik after this three-year assignment. She explained she's been feeling like her life is going around in circles, and this change would give her the good shake she needs. She has already served ten years at this detachment and fears she will soon be transferred anyway. I did some research on the Repulse Bay plight tonight. I must say I would love to bring my contribution to the

Aivilingmiut. I was hoping to stay in Inuvik a while longer, but this uprooting would probably feel quite different if Heidi comes along. Policing remote hamlets was initially what I had in mind when I was fed up with Vancouver, but I do remember how demanding the task is.

MARCH 10, 2005

My sister and I sat down for lunch and had a frank discussion about our new prospect. I reminded Heidi that a two-person detachment workload can be quite overwhelming. While office hours are Monday to Friday from 9 a.m. to 5 p.m., constables are on call twenty-four hours a day and get very little rest. Relief officers would be flown in once in a while so we could get a break, but we would have to brace ourselves for quite a ride.

Heidi had considered that part of the equation; the possibility of a transfer against her will is a matter that is more pressing to her. She wants to start learning Inuktitut right away and asked if I could give her some lessons. We informed Sergeant Matthews of our intentions. He nodded but said he was rather sorry to see us go.

MARCH 14, 2005

A Relocation Reviewer contacted us about housing arrangements this morning. Heidi and I are willing to share a furnished residence and alleviate the community's housing shortage. "The Finance Branch is going to love you," the lady replied. We even proposed to live at the detachment as it used to be done, but the reviewer only laughed at us.

I give Heidi an Inuktitut lesson every day, and she is truly eager to learn. She is well-versed in Inuit social norms, but believes she will not be fit to police the Repulse Bay detachment unless she gains a solid understanding of the local language and culture. She recently admitted she's ill at ease with the fact I was raised by an academic who'd turned me into "a walking encyclopaedia, though it often comes in handy." She feared I perceived her as boorish and thought she made poor conversation. I assured her those thoughts had never crossed my mind. "I don't meet ambidextrous sharpshooters who call bears out on their bluff charges everyday," I said. "I've always esteemed your keen spirit." She didn't think there was anything particular about any of that.

Heidi had never verbalized those thoughts before, but I began perceiving this bashfulness when my mother flew in from Montreal last September. Heidi meant to keep out of sight the whole visit, but I insisted on having her over for dinner once, and my mother wanted to meet her. Heidi was worried about what she should wear and asked if she should come to dinner in her red serge to which I laughed out loud thinking she was in jest. She was not, and she blushed. You would have thought she was about to meet Queen Elizabeth II herself. I got to fully grasp how my sister uses the uniform to conceal real or imaginary shortcomings in knowledge and skill. The constable identity becomes her refuge. Heidi finally showed up in a white blouse and a knee-length grey skirt I had never seen her in before. Her hair was neatly styled into a French twist.

I thought a stranger was standing on my doorstep. I later learned that our detachment's receptionist had helped her with this classy ensemble.

Heidi barely said a word that night and only spoke when spoken to. She kept hunting, trapping and mounted trophies out of our conversation, avoiding any remark the intellectual elite might consider politically incorrect. Heidi remembered everything my mother liked and disliked as not to offend her in any way. My mother was curious to hear what she had to say about the residential school legacy. Heidi offered a few balanced insights, but my mother broke into an impassioned tirade against Christianity, blaming the religion for every evil in the universe (a lecture I've heard time and time again). Heidi did not insist on keeping her own train of thought. "She's a decent young woman," was my mother's verdict once Heidi had left. I nodded but felt sad about my sister's performance. I wished my mother had seen the real Heidi Finlay, but would she have found her half as decent? I did not think so, and that made me even sadder.

Heidi is surprised to have so many people telling her she will be missed. Aluki Kudlak is heartbroken. She does look up to her godmother with much admiration and is considering joining the Force when she turns 19. I told her there is a great need for Inuit constables, and her contribution would be appreciated. Sarah cried when her friend announced she was leaving, but she knew it was bound to happen some day.

MARCH 31, 2005

My sister and I have landed in Repulse Bay tonight. The current temperature is thirty degrees below. We are too tired to undertake anything. Adjusting to the new time zone will take a day or two, but our quarters are quite cozy. The house is decently furnished, and there are bedrooms with a cot for each of us. One of the relief officers gave us a tour of the detachment and introduced us to the overnight detention guard. We got a clearer picture of why the previous officers had been flown out of the hamlet after only six months on the job. Young Constable Kevin Fournier had been shot in a nasty standoff with a drug dealer in February while his partner responded to a domestic disturbance call a few streets away. This had left Fournier to deal with the perilous situation on his own. The wounded officer is still recovering, and the partner has been given a new assignment. This is not reassuring, but the dealer is presently detained at the Baffin Correctional Centre, so we have nothing to fear from him at this point.

The relief officer sounded optimistic when he found out I can speak Inuktitut. He believes this will certainly facilitate our relationship with the Inuit. "You don't look the part, but you speak the part, so that's mighty good news," he said. He and his partner will be running the detachment until the end of the week, granting us some time to settle in and meet with the local people. I was afraid the officer's narrative had scared Heidi off, but she does not seem troubled in the least.

APRIL 1, 2005

We had a major snow storm today. I fell on Heidi's photo album while unpacking and sat down to flip through its pages. I like to look at it once in a while to get a glimpse of what I missed as she was growing up. A picture taken by Roy Elias when Heidi and Sarah were ten shows the girls in early spring on a komatik. Sarah's brother Red, who now lives in Yellowknife, is standing behind them, smiling. Heidi told me she used to envy Sarah because of Red. I asked why. She replied she had once opened up to Sarah about how frightened and restless she sometimes got at night. She had not received much empathy from her friend; nocturnal fears were not a big deal to Sarah, who would join Red, curl up close to him and go back to sleep in no time. Heidi said her mother would let her sleep by her side when she was a young child, but once she reached a certain age, she was expected to show bravery and over-come her fears.

I felt awful sorry and wished I had been there for Heidi when she needed me. I asked her what those fears were. They were many, but one consisted of their home burning down and her mother perishing in the fire, leaving her alone and helpless in the middle of the night. She had a recurring nightmare about going blind and trying to find her way along the Dempster Highway with no passer-by willing to lend her a hand. Urban legends and stories of the paranormal were also sources of great anguish and sleep-less nights.

Heidi inquired about my childhood fears. I immediately remembered watching *The Time Machine* in the seventies and imagining that Morlock creatures lived in a cave outside my room in Yellowknife. I couldn't believe how funny this sounded although it had been a ghastly experience for me as an eight-year-old boy. I also noted I could not dissociate the idea of fear from the daunting events of my parents' divorce; I entered a sinister crevasse of the soul I did not wish to revisit, but Heidi had her arm around me, and there was warmth – both physical and emotional – that brought a light into the menacing place. I believe I described the event in a satisfactory manner, although I could not recall distinct elements the way Heidi had. I remember having a carefree attitude that I was forced to renounce forthwith, my father walking out with his Dall ram trophy and me venturing into the unknown. The ephemeral nature of things had been disclosed to me as a nightmare from which I could not wake. I could only charge and let the various fears fade into abstract forms. I thought Heidi would mock me as she has known much worst in terms of pain and fear, but she did not laugh. I can't imagine what having to watch your mother go mad and try to kill you would ever be like, but these events are off limits, and Heidi rarely ever brings them up.

APRIL 3, 2005

The temperature has considerably warmed up. A friendly young man named Jaycolassie Simik offered to show us around; he works as a tour guide at Ukkusiksalik National Park and took us to the floe edge in a komatik to see the narwhals. The day was windy yet sunny, and we had a wonderful time. The strangeness of the *Monodon monoceros* emerging tusk first always makes for an enthralling spectacle. I shivered in fear and delight as I pondered the waters' hidden depths and the creatures swimming under our feet. "I know you will see ugly and painful things dealing with crime here," Jaycolassie affirmed, "but I wanted you to know Repulse Bay isn't just that."

The man also took us to the cliff where seagulls nest in summertime and from which the hamlet got its Inuktitut name "Naujaat", meaning "seagull fledglings". Our conversation was in Inuktitut, and Jaycolassie was very pleased to hear me speak his language. I asked Heidi if she preferred English, but she wants to get used to Inuktitut and pressed us to keep on so she could learn. She asked our guide where she could go hunting, and he pointed out the best spots. Jaycolassie Simik displays a strong sense of belonging to this hamlet and seems truly invested in his people's well-being. He looks at what could be and not only at what is. I hope to meet many more like him here.

APRIL 5, 2005

Living with my sister is a refreshing experience. We did not get to grow up together, but are now sharing the same roof and discovering each other's habits. Heidi walked into the laundry room as I sorted our garments into four baskets today. She watched like one fascinated. She seemed to consider the practice rather unusual, so I asked if she washes her underwear and tea towels separately. "I never saw the need," she replied. We had an engrossing conversation on the possibility of *E. Coli* and *Staphylococcus aureus* bacteria spreading into the water from our underwear and finding their way onto our uniforms and kitchen utensils.

"Who taught you to do this?" she asked. I explained how my mother had obtained this information from a colleague at Concordia's science department and how she'd passed this laundry technique down to me. Heidi was so entertained, she laughed heartily.

"Do you make sure your water temperature is at least 40 degrees Celsius and 60 when you have a cold?" I inquired. She does not. She does not even care to wash colours separately but usually throws everything into a single load and lets it whirl around in cold water on the normal cycle. Now, that came across as gross negligence to me. I considered asking about Duncan Forrester's techniques since he had a solid reputation as a clean man, but I didn't because I know Heidi's former husband is a delicate subject, and she doesn't like to talk about him.

Heidi was delighted to come across an intact caribou skull in our neighbour's yard yesterday. She asked a teenager who lives there if she could keep it. He looked at her in a funny way but nodded, and she hung it in her bedroom, saying it evoked plenty of her fondest childhood memories. There is something creepy about Heidi when it comes to hunting and carcasses. There are associations happening in her head I will never understand. I suppose growing up watching your Inuvialuit guardians skinning animals will do this to you.

APRIL 6, 2005

We received a sobering phone call in the early morning hours. Seventeen-year-old Jack Tagalik had hung himself in a closet while his family was sound asleep. His cousins found his body as they went looking for clothes for the school day. There are no social workers in Naujaat at the moment, and I had to sit with Jack's parents and siblings and act as a grief counsellor. The younger children were confused while the older ones cried. The Tagaliks are a large family, and with the housing shortage, eighteen of them are presently living in a four-bedroom house. Each bedroom contains two or three mattresses spread on the floor for everyone to sleep on, and the walls and windows are considerably damaged. Building materials are hard to come by in these parts. It was difficult to find a quiet place to sit for our discussion.

Mrs Tagalik would not open up and preferred to be left alone with her children, wondering how a stranger like me could be of any help to them. Heidi took upon herself to conduct the investigation and rule out any possibility of homicide in her cold-blooded manner. She likes to think of herself as pragmatic, although I know she is not uncaring; she wears her heart in her pocket, not on her sleeve. We sure didn't expect to deal with a suicide during our very first week in Naujaat. Heidi is getting the shake she needed all right, but I don't think it is the kind of shaking she originally had in mind.


APRIL 8, 2005

An anonymous tip led to the arrest of one Jim Kusugak this afternoon. The young man had small amounts of cocaine and hashish in his possession, and a snowmobile search revealed empty packages suggesting ongoing drug trafficking. He is presently held in our cell block, and Heidi brought him his supper an hour ago. He uses colourful language as a way of protest and threw a few insults at her when she approached his cell. She stared through the window in this unsettling way of hers that makes you feel like she can see right through you. She did not have to say a word to quiet him down, and this is something that always impresses me. Some policemen wear their uniform like a second skin; the first thing people see when they look at them is the power vested in them, and they shake. Heidi Finlay inspires precisely that. I don't see my sister in this way myself, but I have noticed it is the effect she has on many.

I asked Heidi how she likes her experience so far. "I miss the bush," was her only complaint. The absence of trees startles her. The stark tundra does have a way of making you feel vulnerable, and I am always in awe of the Inuit's ingenuity when I stop to think about it. Who were those men and women who first managed to survive the Arctic desert armed with uluit, kudliks and igluit?

Having the sea so close at hand is a pleasant novelty, and it is obviously embraced as a great wealth in Naujaat. Heidi will soon get her fishing and hunting licenses and this will hopefully reduce the grocery bill. A small bag of flour goes for thirty dollars at the Northern Store. Heidi's game could perhaps provide for some impoverished families in the community. I hear many of them can barely make ends meet.

APRIL 11, 2005

A second suicide case was brought to my attention this morning; Victor Killiktee, 19, shot himself last night with an unregistered firearm a kilometre away from the hamlet. I was able to confirm Victor had indeed taken his own life. His family and friends all spoke of a severe cocaine addiction and how the young man had shown indisputable signs of depression in recent weeks.

Heidi was on another call for a suicide attempt by suffocation and met a nurse from the health centre who told her three women had been admitted for the same reason last month. One of them had been sexually assaulted the year before, and due to a housing shortage, had had no other choice but to keep living with her abuser. "I feel for them, Jasper," Heidi said. "Being stuck in a crowded home would be the death of me. And sharing it with someone I fear on top of that! I'd be choking for air and space." All in all, there have been six suicides and eight attempts in Naujaat since January for a hamlet of some 700 souls. This overwhelming trend is seen all over the territory; the Government of Nunavut implemented a suicide prevention strategy last year, but its tangible impact remains to be seen.

APRIL 12, 2005

I dropped by the Co-op for a bite at noon and met a talented carver named Joe Irniq. The middle-aged man works mainly with serpentine, and his sculptures are on display in the cooperative's glass case along with those of a dozen local artists. He had come to add three more to the collection, one of which represented a walrus lying on its side. The soapstone's brown tone made Irniq's creation life-like, and I purchased it from him in honour of the Aivilingmiut, the "people of the walrus place". I asked if he had eaten. He agreed to have lunch with me and talk about his techniques. My uniform made him nervous at first, but once I'd told him about my father's collection, his tongue was freed.

Joe works exclusively with hand tools, as he dislikes the noise of power tools and the amount of dust they leave everywhere. He asked a few questions about my police work. I mentioned the suicide issue, and the carver nodded, looking away as if staring into the eyes of a painful memory. Joe Irniq had contemplated suicide on three occasions as a young man; he said there was deep confusion as to who he was and who his people were and where they were all going. Carving had allowed him to find his identity as an Inuit. He brought his traditions and the animals associated with them to life in his art. When an Australian tourist had purchased a polar bear sculpture from him one summer, he'd felt great joy and a sense of accomplishment that someone had travelled from so far away to visit his hamlet, explore his culture and bring a piece of it with him down under. "I felt I was worth something," he said. "I felt like my people had a right to exist and were meant to exist. I hope those youngsters can come to appreciate who we are and not take their lives in a moment of despair."

I asked if the pieces he carves help define his people through a kind of symbolism. He nodded again and offered me a bright, toothless smile. Joe Irniq believes Naujaat's youth are torn between two worlds – the traditional Inuit ways and modern realities – and they don't know where to go from there. He wishes there were more hunting expeditions to reinforce the traditions and to help feed the hamlet, but high fuel and food prices make such expeditions costly and only a few can afford them.

APRIL 14, 2005

A new tragedy hit the Tagalik household today. Jack Tagalik's fourteen-year-old cousin Silas hung himself in the bathroom and was found by his uncle in the morning. We discovered that Silas' older sister Elisapie was murdered by her abusive boyfriend in Baker Lake two years ago, making the loss even heavier for the family. Silas' ten-year-old sister, Alasie, was sobbing uncontrollably, as in a state of panic. The child was born with leg length discrepancy and suffers intimidation at school. Silas' uncle told us her brother was very protective of her, leaving her feeling like she had now lost her shield.

I sensed abashment as the Tagaliks wondered what they were doing wrong and how they could have prevented Jack and Silas' deaths. Postvention is crucial in this case since imitative suicidal behaviour seems to be taking root, but the Tagaliks are still unreceptive to counselling.

APRIL 18, 2005

Heidi and I awoke to a succession of rifle shots at four o'clock this morning. We dressed quickly, and as Heidi looked out the window with her revolver in hand, another shot came, breaking the glass and missing her by a few centimetres. I grabbed my sister and pulled her to the ground. We had not been in Naujaat long enough to make enemies. Who was this gunman and why was he attacking us personally? We heard voices and neighbours gathering, begging one Levi Kidlapik to stop and surrender his weapon. The confrontation lasted an hour during which the assailant fired five more times at the house as I attempted dialogue through the broken window. Kidlapik would not speak to us for the longest time until he shot once in the air, screaming: "Come out here!" angrily.

"What is your request?" I asked.

"Come out here, both of you!"

At this point, a valiant man by the name of Joanasie Anguk pushed Kidlapik in the snow and succeeded in taking the firearm away from him, making a citizen's arrest. Heidi and I rushed outside and handcuffed the drunken man who broke down and cried all the way to the detachment. As much as he'd frightened us half to death a moment before, we felt rather sorry for him at this point; Kidlapik was having an anxiety attack. Heidi filed a report in the office while I stayed with the man in his cell, trying to find out what had happened and what his motivations were. He would not answer my questions. When I brought him breakfast three hours later, he apologized and explained he had attacked us in the hope that we would kill him in self-defence. Kidlapik's girlfriend had broken up with him the night before, and he wanted to die so badly. "I meant no harm," he said. "I'm a good shot and could have killed you both if I wanted to. I didn't."

I am still very much shaken. I made Heidi promise she would always call me for backup if she had to deal with violent offenders here. I wonder if agreeing to this transfer was a good decision after all. The risk is so high with only two constables to handle every call. It frightens me to look back and recognize how lonely I was before I discovered I had a sister. I would not want to lose her and face that lonesomeness once more.

APRIL 20, 2005

A noteworthy event which brought both joy and wonder took place tonight, and I still don't know what to make of it. As we drove back to the detachment after answering a domestic disturbance call, a crowd began to gather out on the bay. We pulled over to investigate and discovered a heap of illicit drugs, pornographic magazines and heavy metal recordings rising higher and higher as the Aivilingmiut rushed back and forth to add their contribution to the mound. I asked a man what they intended to do with this. "We are going to burn it," he answered. "We are coming clean before the Lord."

I made a brief assessment and found they were planning to destroy some $40,000 worth of material. I told myself I was surely asleep and dreaming, so I turned to ask my sister to shake me. Heidi was speaking to one of the community elders. She walked back to our cruiser, took the gas can from the trunk and offered it to the man who gladly poured the fuel onto the pile. Matches were thrown in, the heap inflamed; a thick, dark smoke rose into the air and was soon carried away towards the sea as we stepped back to contemplate the merry bonfire.

What sort of impact will this have on the hamlet? I have often seen how the interception of a bootlegger's shipment can prevent violence in dry towns; hopefully the drugs destroyed will ease the strife in Naujaat for the weeks to come.

The weather was cloudy and mild today, and I went out for a walk after lunch. I met young Alasie Tagalik on my way to the bay. I recognized her unique gait and walked up to her to ask how she was coping. A massive husky dog followed closely behind but left her side and ran to me as I approached the pair. He began sniffing my coat pocket, and I remembered leaving a bag of Heidi's moose jerky in there the day before. "Is that your dog, Alasie?" I asked. She said it was their neighbour's dog, Nukilik, but her family looked after him while the owners were away in Iqaluit.

"Give me your hand," I said. "Here's something for your pal."

She took her mitten off, and I poured a handful of jerky in it for the craving animal. Alasie wore a lovely spotted sealskin anorak with a pointy hood, and I complimented her on it.

"My grandmother made it," she replied. Her brothers and sister had all worn it before her.

Could she eat some of the jerky I had given her? I gave her some more and inquired if she was hungry. She shrugged and looked down with a kind of shame. I asked how she was feeling. "Fine" was her evasive answer. She was as reluctant as her mother and aunt to talk, but I told her she could come to the detachment at any time for a chat. She nodded and limped away. I am planning to go to

Tusarvik on a school day to observe how the bullying issue is manifested on the playground and in the halls.

Heidi agreed to run the detachment office on her own this morning, so I could go to Tusarvik, meet the teachers and see if we could get involved with the Drug Abuse Resistance Education program. I chose not to wear my uniform as it influences youngsters to act differently around me. I wanted a true glimpse of the student dynamic in Naujaat, so I sat down on a stone a few steps away from the playground. I spotted Alasie Tagalik soon enough; she walked close to the wall and mostly kept to herself. A few girls her age looked at her with certain pity as she limped passed them, and I suppose they didn't have a clue about how to tackle her profound grief. Alasie had brought a book from which she looked up once in a while; her attention was directed at a tall boy who stood at the opposite side of the schoolyard. He was a few years older than Alasie and looked somewhat familiar to me. "The looser is back," he shouted once he'd noticed how she repeatedly glanced at him with apprehension. I am assuming the girl had been away from school following her brother's death, and the boy had not seen her since. He walked straight to Alasie, snatched the book from her hands and threw it violently against the wall. He sneered as if he delighted in her fear and in the power he had over her.

"I would advise you to stop and apologize immediately, young man," I said.

The boy turned around and frowned.

"Who the hell are you?" he asked, insolently.

"Constable Jasper Nelson, Royal Canadian Mounted Police."

The boy stared in anger and uttered a word I will not transcribe here. A teacher later explained I had confronted Jim Kusugak's younger brother Saul. The boy obviously resented me for arresting his sibling, who had a rather questionable influence on him. I am told Saul Kusugak is held back and skips school regularly. Tusarvik's personnel think of him as a lost cause and have run out of ideas to help him mend his ways. I am worried for Alasie. I know her teachers also have to act as grief counsellors in our present situation; they do offer support, but Alasie is withdrawn and refuses to talk though she is a good enough student. She is occasionally protected by compassionate classmates who feel Saul Kusugak should "pick on someone his size".

I had just introduced Tusarvik's principal to the DARE program when Heidi called me for back-up about a suicide attempt involving a firearm. I left in a hurry and joined her at the caller's residence. Loud music was playing in the house, and we entered through the back door unnoticed. A young woman in tears was holding a hunting rifle and threatening to take her own life with her mother begging her not to. "Let me go!" she cried. "I'm a failure; you will all be better off without me." I snuck up from behind, knocked the weapon out of the girl's hands and took her to the health centre for treatment.

I am not used to this sort of policing. What a lie these victims believe to think their departure from this world will make life easier for their loved ones! The brokenness and perplexity they leave behind is inexpressible. I am also seeing how this sets an example for others to follow, and it is this aspect which frightens me the most. The situation has clearly reached the level of contagion.

APRIL 27, 2005

When and how will this ever stop? Alasie Tagalik hung herself by the neck on a rope she had tied to the Inns North's satellite dish today. She was found by the hotel manager at first light, and she had been hanging there for at least two hours. He was so horrified he didn't dare to cut her down, and Heidi and I had to do it ourselves. My sister could not keep it in this time, and we both wept bitterly. Mrs Tagalik is inconsolable. Some of her neighbours are accusing her of not loving her children enough and are imposing a burden of guilt she cannot bear at the moment. Everyone is puzzled at how young Alasie learned to tie a hangman's noose.

I feel powerless.

APRIL 30, 2005

Heidi got her small game hunting licence and shot five hares today. She wanted to share her game with the Tagaliks, thinking they could certainly use the extra meat with so many mouths to feed. We were welcomed by Jack Tagalik's older sister, Rachel. She lives in Baker Lake, and we had not met before. Heidi asked me to do the talking as she is not yet comfortable with Inuktitut conversation. Rachel Tagalik did not expect me to know her language;

she gave Heidi a suspicious look when I explained she had killed the animals herself.

"My sister was raised on the trapline in Inuvik," I explained. "She is a skilled shooter and learned her techniques from her Inuvialuit guardians." Rachel's attitude changed; she had taken for granted we were both Southerners who knew nothing about their way of life. Rachel Tagalik had a surprisingly cynical outlook on the recent hardships befalling her kin. I believe the repetitive blows had stiffened her heart to such a degree she simply expected things to get worse until there was nothing left.

"Is there anything we can do to help?" I asked.

"I don't really see how Mounties could be of any help. It's not your job."

"It's not part of our work description, but we have been forced to handle these situations because of a lack of social workers. We are left wondering what we could do better to prevent more deaths in the community."

"Some say our family is cursed. Some of us have begun to believe it… Do you think we are cursed?"

"I think the first to take his life set an example for others to follow. They began to believe the lie that killing oneself is the only way out of despair."

"Resources are scarce. What people need is hope. But we are out of sight and out of mind up here. Living in remote locations has its price tag. Even those who'd rather move don't have the money to do it. We are left to our own devices. I suppose there was hope when the new territory was born. We thought we would succeed. We thought we could make it better on our own and in our own way. Things only seem to be deteriorating."

"It may take some time for things to get better," I said.

"It's too late for all of them," she replied.

Rachel Tagalik looked up; her face expressed clear resentment towards us. Heidi perceived it as well as me. She believes the young woman associates us with the various ills white men have brought to her people through the decades, disturbing their ways of life and introducing poisons Inuit cannot yet handle properly. She is mistrustful and strongly believes in "solutions by Inuit for Inuit", but unlike her mother, seems to acknowledge a need for outside help. She thanked us for the meat yet left us feeling like pries offering cough drops to a cancer patient. And perhaps we were.

I later found Heidi curled up on the sofa, her face half-buried in the rabbit fur throw she'd brought over from Inuvik.

"Can you feel that heaviness?" she asked.

"I am rather disheartened, yes."

"Are we failing big time, Jasper?"

"Our intervention seems inadequate. But I believe much of this is beyond our control."

"Is it only social issues? Is there something more at play? An oppressive force pushing people over the edge?"

"What do you mean?"

"I'm not sure. I don't understand it. But I think those people do. Those people who burned their things. They're fighting on a different level... It's a battle for souls."

I suppose my sister was referring to the notion of spiritual warfare. Sergeant Matthews had introduced her to this idea after a possessed man confronted us in her hunting cabin five years ago. She has been sensitive to the spiritual dimension ever since. Aboriginal people do see spirituality as an integral part of their healing process. They find the white man's approach lacking as it does not take those matters into account. We have gradually rejected them to the point of thinking they have no relevance at all. Material elements can be arranged and rearranged to no end; an inner nature that remains unchanged will keep causing havoc that external improvements cannot stop.

"I will get supper ready," I said.

"Don't make anything for me. I want to fast."

Heidi retired to her room and went to bed early.

I am baffled as I write these words. Diligence and goodwill have proven insufficient so far, and I am at a loss as to how to do my work effectively from now on.

M A Y   1 ,   2 0 0 5

Naujaat is a mysterious place; a wondrous thing happened tonight as we headed home after a stroll along the bay. A sound of music and Inuktitut singing rang ever clearer as we approached a plain white building easily mistaken for a snowy knoll in the distance. A thin brown cross and an inscription indicated we had stumbled upon Naujaat's Glad Tidings church where a service was being held. The spring air was still, yet it appeared that a strong wind and a roll of thunder had filled the building and shaken it to its foundations. We stared wide-eyed for a moment. Much to my surprise, Heidi was deeply moved and exclaimed: "Come on!" as she pulled me into the low-ceiling sanctuary where an Inuit congregation wept and prayed with its hands up in the air. The musicians had put their instruments down, trying to make sense of what they were hearing. I was just as perplexed and joined the young man standing by the sound system. He had turned everything off, thinking there was something wrong with the speakers, but the sound of the rushing wind kept getting louder and louder. Many were now on their knees saying: "Holy Spirit, come down, come down!" Heidi was wiping tears off her cheeks, standing side by side with an old man we had repeatedly arrested for public intoxication. He was pressing a rumpled New Testament to his chest and asking for deliverance. This lasted a few minutes, and the noise slowly receded, leaving a contemplative silence behind it.

Heidi said nothing at all on the way home. I thought I would have to drag an explanation out of her until she whispered: "It has lifted."

"What has lifted?" I asked.

"Couldn't you sense that oppression? The hamlet was full of it."

I admitted the succession of suicides had indeed plunged Naujaat in deep consternation, but what she was referring to was rather abstract and spiritual in nature.

"You cried with that drunkard," I said. "Why?"

"Something got a hold of me... I'm no better than him."

That was a strange declaration, but Heidi spoke with conviction. She believes a difference was made tonight. She did not expound, as if she feared I would not understand nor take her seriously. I now know it is useless to force Heidi to talk until she has processed her thoughts, and I am willing to wait for her to point out that difference as she sees it unfold.

MAY 10, 2005

Child suicide leaves no one indifferent. Alasie Tagalik's death shook Naujaat to its core, and I heard an old man in the street declare: "We have to sit down and talk about it." I find this reassuring, as silence only perpetuates the bleeding and leaves the suicidal with no other option but to execute their plan.

There has not been any suicides since Alasie's two weeks ago. Heidi is not getting her hopes up but says she has the impression one gets when the thick cloud cover dissipates after a storm.

I ran into Saul Kusugak's teacher at the Co-op yesterday. I asked how he reacted to Alasie's death. Many of his classmates are holding him responsible, and he is in a state of shock. You cannot mess with matches every day without getting burned or setting the house on fire. Ms. Stuart found him unusually introspective, and we are both confident this affliction will help turn his life around.

MAY 11, 2005

We met a young mother carrying a baby boy in her amauti this morning. We smiled at them, and as I pondered this new life full of promise, Heidi chuckled.

"What's so funny?" I asked. "Are you laughing at them?"

"I'm laughing at myself, actually," she replied.

She told me that when Aluki Kudlak was born, Sarah had once asked her to baby-sit and explained how to use the amauti if she wanted to go for a walk. Heidi had never worn such a garment and badly wanted to try it. Sarah is considerably plumper than Heidi, and the parka did not fit my sister too well. Once her friend was gone, she had set Aluki into the pouch, but the baby had slipped into her sleeve and was struggling to escape. "I'm laughing now, but I wasn't laughing then," Heidi said. "I was praying so hard! I thought she would choke, and I was very afraid of squishing her. You should have seen me dance around the living room, trying to get her out of there!" Aluki eventually found her way back up, popping a dishevelled head out of the pouch to Heidi's great relief.

I asked Heidi if she plans to have children some day. She had begun discussing this with her husband when he got in trouble and left. It took her a while to get over Duncan Forrester's dissimulations. She doesn't know if she'll marry again and says she has a hard time trusting people now.

"What makes you trust people?" I inquired.

She paused to think about it.

"Do you trust me?"

"I do."

"Why?"

"I think you've earned it," she answered.

May has been characterized by light but regular snowfall so far, and the temperature has not yet risen above zero. Sarah Kudlak called the other day and told us Inuvik is in full flood mode, and everybody is walking around in their rubber boots. For some odd reason, Heidi and I felt very low after hearing this and wished we could fly over for a visit.

My baby sister turned thirty years old today. We have not yet made close friends to speak of, so I could not think of anyone to invite, but I baked a cake, and we had a nice supper of arctic char together. Sugar tends to have an exhilarating effect on Heidi, and she declared: "Well, now that we are both official members of the Old Fogies Association, I say we complete our three years here in Repulse Bay, resign and retire to my cabin in Inuvik. I'll go trapping, and you can grow a beard and read to your heart's content. If you ever feel bored, you could volunteer your skills to the local search and rescue teams. How's that sound?"

"Sounds like a plan," I said, "But you are too young to join the Association."

"Nonsense. It's an attitude thing. I'm nobody's fool, and I daresay I have reached a higher level than you have at this."

"I'll grant you that."

Heidi was in jest, but I know leaving the Force and going back to the bush is an idea she brings up once in a while, and she means to do it one day. I asked if she really plans to retire early.

"I do feel like I'm over the hill," she answered. "Maybe it's the exhaustion. It's not physical, but it's the feeling of having seen more death and depravity than you ever expected in your lifetime. Don't you feel the need to get away from it all at times?"

I nodded. I can relate to this, but it appears to be a more persisting feeling for Heidi.

"This world makes less and less sense to me," she affirmed.

You would think these words to be those of a despondent mind, but she was at peace about it, as if this was a meaningful place to start and get to work.

"It's broken," she went on. "We're all broken. That's where redemption becomes indispensable. That's where we can start afresh. We all need to die first, but not in the way these people have. I see it now; this misery is fertile ground for those who really want redemption."

"You think that's what happened at Glad Tidings that night?'

Heidi nodded.

Days are getting longer, and the midnight sun should be seen in a week from now. Exploring the Naujaat shore has become a staple part of this assignment, and we went for our evening stroll after supper. We met walrus hunters hauling an impressive catch out on the bay. The men chatted away with great pride as they parted the meat between the families waiting with their plastic bags and boxes ready. My face must have brightened up at this sight because Heidi squeezed my arm and said: "You *will* get your ideal sometimes, Jasper."

# WHERE DUTY LIES
## (CONSTABLE FINLAY)

When I was twenty and completing my RCMP training in Regina, I met a journalism student at a classmate's party a week before Christmas. He was somewhat tipsy and kept jabbering about a CIA mind-control experiment conducted on unwitting patients at a Montreal hospital in the 1960's. The tests described sounded very much like torture. We had vaguely heard of the victims' lawsuit on the news in recent years, but this young man insisted the research had been funded by our own government. It was an awkward conversation, and we were all thinking the student had bought into a wild conspiracy theory. We still felt uneasy about the possible truth behind his tale, but took comfort in the belief that these things mostly happen in major cities or in the United States of America anyway. We brushed it off and had forgotten all about it by the time we'd resumed our training in January.

As an Arctic child raised on the trapline in Inuvik, I did not feel concerned and thought of my town as a safe haven. My perceptions have changed over time. I am writing this sitting by the stove in my hunting cabin in the bush, thinking there is no safe place and that men of good will are a scarce commodity in this fallen world. You might read my tale and think of me as I thought of the Regina student. Well, I have come to value truth above social approbation.

The time is November 5, 2008. A light snow is falling, and the days are growing shorter, pointing to the polar night that is soon to come upon us. My brother Jasper Nelson is sitting on the sofa, flipping through a crumpled copy of the Criminal Code. I believe it is fair to say we are both in a state of shock and confusion, even more so for my brother who is kind and trusting and had always held our country's institutions in high esteem. It is strange to no longer think of ourselves as constables of the Royal Canadian Mounted Police, because that is what we still were only a month ago.

IT ALL BEGAN on an August night when Constable Frank Winston of the Inuvik detachment was called to an accident scene on the Dempster Highway, four kilometres away from town. The call originated from one of the drivers – one Gordon Miller who described the crash and said the Inuvialuit woman who drove the second car was unconscious. No charges were laid, and Winston's report stated the collision was due to poor visibility. My brother and I knew nothing of this case until my friend Sarah Kudlak called at the detachment to tell me the injured woman wished to speak to an officer about the incident. The victim, her cousin Ann Nasogaluak, had been released from the hospital where she'd been treated for broken ribs and multiple leg fractures. I drove up to her house on the west side of town. Sarah let me in and led me to the kitchen where the woman sat with one leg held up on a chair. She looked me over with suspicion. Ann had probably hoped to see our Inuvialuit corporal "Grizzly" Alunik, but Sarah assured her I could be trusted.

"Maybe you can tell me why the Mountie who dealt with this crash lied and let a criminal go free," she mumbled, impatiently.

Ann was outraged to hear the collision had been ruled out as a weather-related accident, and the man who'd nearly killed her had not been charged with impaired driving. She was adamant visibility was excellent that night, and Miller's erratic driving clearly indicated alcohol or drug consumption. Ann was suggesting Frank Winston's report had covered up a crime, and he'd possibly been bribed to do so. That was a disturbing notion. I didn't know what to say but suggested she lodge a complaint and promised to do what I could about it.

I located Winston's report at the detachment. The name Gordon Miller rang a bell, but I couldn't quite remember where I had heard it. My brother happened to walk by my desk and I said:

"Jasper, do you know any Gordon Miller?"

"Gordon Miller? ...The ring-tapping lawyer?"

"Ring-tapping?"

"He's one of the defense lawyers at the Territorial Court. He often taps his pinky finger ring during trial, almost as if he's signalling something to the judge. I've often wondered if it means anything or if it's only a tic."

The picture of a heavy, blue-eyed man with a short grey beard arose in my mind.

"Yes, I remember now... Is that the same Gordon Miller who was involved in a car accident on August 20?"

"I believe so. I heard he suffered some minor injuries and couldn't show up in court. What is this about?"

I told him. Jasper proceeded to consult weather records, confirming there had not been any fog or precipitations in our area that night. We were rather puzzled. Nothing unusual or twisted about the winsome Frank had ever come to our attention, but we had only met him a few months earlier. Winston had been assigned to the Inuvik detachment while my brother and I lived in Repulse Bay and policed the two-person detachment for three years. His first posting had been down in Langley, British Columbia. He is fairly young and on his way to being promoted to corporal, which shows great ambition on his part.

The phone rang and I had to put this file away. Jasper came back later in the afternoon. He sat by my desk and drew a quick sketch of a square and compass joined together with a capital G in between.

"The Freemasons?"

"Ever noticed Winston's signet ring?"

"Winston's a Mason?"

Jasper had gone to the kitchen to get some coffee and met Winston there. The young man was chatting with Corporal Alunik and held his cup to his mouth once in a while, showing this particular jewel worn on the ring finger.

"I did some reading. You need to be a Master Mason to obtain one of these rings."

"He means business about it… Is this the same kind of ring Gordon Miller owns and keeps tapping at the judge?"

"I intend to get a closer look and find out. I have to testify in court on Friday. Miller's defending Sadek. I suggest we keep quiet about this until then."

And that is what we did. I worked the evening shift on Friday, but still came to court and sat close to Gordon Miller in the public seating area in the hope of seeing his ring. The accused was one Adnan Sadek, a restaurant owner who sells drugs and alcohol from his home on the side. We raided his house in 1999, and he had shot me at close range under the left clavicle. I am lucky he hit my vest; a few centimetres higher, and I'd be riding the pale horse. He got eight years for assaulting a peace officer but was released after two; he'd used a legally owned bird-hunting shotgun and claimed he'd aimed at my vest "on purpose". He'd panicked but meant no harm. He got himself a fine for the bootlegging part. Jasper was incensed. Sadek resumed his illegal activities upon returning to Inuvik.

Last April, my brother surprised an Inuvialuit teenager knocking on Sadek's back window. She was turned away by Sadek who'd told her he had nothing to offer at the moment. Jasper spoke to the girl, and in his compassionate manner, made her admit she had come for salvia, which she'd purchased from the dealer before. My brother kept an eye on the house and saw this sort of scene recurring several times in the following days. A search warrant led us to 23 mickeys of vodka, 100 grams of marijuana, 200 grams of salvia, three restricted weapons and $2,400 in cash. You would think Sadek's jig was up, but it's never that simple.

We all stood, Judge Philip Meyer walked in, and Adnan Sadek had the gall to plead not guilty.

"Constable Nelson, could you describe what you saw Mr. Sadek do on April the 6th at two o'clock in the afternoon?" the Crown Prosecutor asked after presenting some extensive evidence.

"I was on patrol downtown when Mr. Sadek walked into the Inuvik liquor store. I saw him exit the establishment with two reusable grocery bags filled with large Smirnoff vodka bottles. He left the bags in the trunk of his car and returned to buy a case of mickey bottles he added to the rest. I then saw him drive away towards a house on Boot Lake Road."

"You followed him?"

"I did, yes."

"Is this Mr. Sadek's personal residence?"

"It is."

Jasper told of the many youths and alcoholics banned from the liquor store he'd later seen knocking on Sadek's back window to purchase various drugs and vodka. An Inuvialuk whose younger brother is one of Sadek's regular customers was also called to the stand. He stated how the boy had quickly sunk into addiction after getting his first taste of Sadek's stock.

"Objection!" Miller cried. "Irrelevant."

"Sustained."

The Defense was allowed to present its case.

"Your honour," Miller began, "the Defense will prove beyond a doubt that the charges laid against my client are the result of a serious misunderstanding. Many of these accusations are unsubstantiated and potentially defamatory. I trust everything will be clarified once it is appropriately dealt with in this court of law."

Witnesses were cross-examined, and many assertions about Sadek using the alcohol for his restaurant were brought forth. Downplaying the large amounts of drugs and restricted firearms was a tougher sell, and the resulting argumentation was ludicrous to say the least. As the defendant answered the Crown Prosecutor's questions, I noticed how Gordon Miller exchanged glances with Judge Meyer. The ring tapping game began. Judge Meyer responded with a slight nod. In spite of the abundant evidence presented, all charges against Adnan Sadek were stayed, and the bootlegger walked out a free man.

I don't believe anger is the best word to describe how Jasper and I felt. Dismay is a better one. We were left wondering if the court system was a farce and what purpose it served except giving the Canadian people an illusion of justice. Gordon Miller passed by me on his way out. I looked straight at his right hand and recognized the square and compass symbol on the gold ring he wore on his pinky finger. Jasper told me he'd also been able to identify it earlier on. To say we were fired up would be an understatement.

After days of sifting through all sorts of cryptic documentation online, Jasper and I learned that Inuvik's masonic lodge, known to insiders as "Far North Lodge 199", held its regular meetings on the second Thursday of each month at 7:30 p.m. In his fervour for truth and justice, my brother determined he would go on a stakeout on his personal time and see who showed up for the occasion. I offered to keep him company. He asked Sarah Kudlak if he could borrow her car since it is black and discreet and Constable Winston would not recognize it. Sarah agreed to help, but did not hand her keys over without some trepidation. We observed an unusual number of visitors in town on that second Thursday in September, and later understood they'd come from various towns and cities for the masonic meeting, covering considerable distances to be in attendance.

Jasper and I both worked the day shift, but our paperwork kept us in the office until seven o'clock. We hurried home to change, and Jasper parked Sarah's car some ten metres away from the lodge. The meeting had already begun. Inuvik's masonic lodge isn't much to look at; it is a small, sky-blue building hidden behind clumps of bushes on Duck Lake Street. You can see Boot Lake beyond. You wouldn't know anything particular is happening there save for the square and compass insignia affixed to the façade, which is the size of a hand and can easily be missed. Jasper was sitting at the wheel, keeping watch on the lodge from his binoculars, when I joined him. I sat on the passenger seat and handed him some of what I had brought for supper –four pieces of dry whitefish and a buttered bannock bun. I split it in two and gave the largest half to my brother.

"I wish my mother had learned this recipe," he said, munching on his bread with a smile.

Back when the Nelsons lived in Yellowknife, Jane Dennett had experimented with local cuisine. Her bannock had turned up as a salty, toasted stone, and Jasper had always disliked bannock because of this. He changed his mind once he got a taste of Vi Elias' recipe. "Maybe your mother was too rough on the kneading," I said when I first heard about this. "That will make the bannock as stiff as a board." Jasper's surprise had turned to chuckles as he'd recounted Jane Dennett's zeal for giving her dough a "good spanking."

We kept quiet while we ate, observing the blue building for a while, but it got boring and Jasper began talking about his dreams, a subject he likes to discuss with me. I don't mind it. It can be rather entertaining, and his dreams are usually much stranger and more colourful than mine. He told me about the time he'd dreamed our father had decided to come look for me.

"When was that?" I asked.

"A few months after the divorce. Dad announced I had a sister, and I could accompany him to Inuvik to meet you if I wished."

"What did you say to that?"

"I was livid. I couldn't believe he had known you existed all this time and hadn't done a single thing about it. I was aware that what he'd done was wrong and had somehow contributed to the divorce, so I wasn't sure I wanted to have anything to do with it. I could tell Dad was feeling guilty and knew he had set a bad example for me. He mumbled I didn't have to come, but I got furious and said I wanted to see you. So, we flew over to Inuvik. It was some time in the fall. It started snowing, and the road got mighty slippery. The taxi driver was doing his best, but the car ended up at the bottom of the Mackenzie River."

"What?"

"We managed to swim to the surface. A nice Inuvialuk offered us a ride on his dogsled, and we reached your mother's house by nightfall. There was a green armchair there, and your mother made me sit in it, asking if I wanted to hold you. She'd built the strangest crib for you and laid it by the stove. It was made out of moose antlers and muskrat skulls she'd nailed together into an oval shape, and you were buried under a heap of pelts. All I could see was a bundle of fur until she laid you in my arms. I had a quick glimpse of your face, then I woke up."

"Muskrat skulls? Why am I always a child in your dreams?"

"Not always."

"Do you often dream about things from the past?"

"Sometimes. But the timeline doesn't always make sense."

Jasper tells me he often has dreams about chasing felons around Inuvik, then remembers he has to stop by a house to make sure a certain child is safe out there. He fears the child's mother will hurt her. By the time he gets to the house, he understands these people are really my mother and me. He sometimes reaches the place by the end of his dream, but he is an adult and I am very young. I believe these have to do with a picture of me as a five-year-old that Jasper framed and hung on his wall shortly after being transferred to Inuvik. Seeing it everyday has enabled him to create these images in his mind. He says my face is clear enough at times, but not that of my mother who remains an elusive figure in every dream.

"My dreams usually happen in the present," I said. "But once I dreamed about us being kids."

"You did?"

"I was about six in that dream. You'd travelled from Vancouver with Dad on a hunting trip. I'd heard you would come to our school for the day, and I was very eager to meet you. You were hanging out with the older boys in the playground, and I attempted to talk to you, but I could never get your attention. Those boys were loud and rough, and I wouldn't dare to speak up. Then a teacher came by, took my hand and asked me to follow her. At recess, some grizzly bears ventured onto school property, and we had to hide inside. I tried to seize every opportunity to see you, but by the end of the day, my efforts had been fruitless. I was heading home disappointed when I found you alone in the playground. I called out to you and you turned around. By the look you gave me, I could tell you knew too. You knew who I was and what I wanted, but you said: 'I'm sorry, I need to go.' And you left."

Jasper stared for a while.

"What an awful dream! Why was I avoiding you like that?"

"You weren't avoiding me. You know how it is with dreams, when all sorts of things get in the way and you can never reach your goal."

"What were you trying to tell me? That you'd found out I was your brother?"

"No, you knew that already. I wanted you to stay. I knew it wasn't really up to us, but I needed to ask... I badly wanted you to stay in Inuvik and not go back to Vancouver."

"Why did you dream that?"

"I don't know. That was several years ago."

"I wouldn't have walked away from you... Why would you dream that about me?"

"Jasper, it's a silly dream."

"That meant something to you."

I didn't want this talk to wax sentimental, but my brother kept insisting and brought me back to a painful place.

"That dream came a few months after you'd moved to Inuvik. It dawned on me that our work in the Force would likely separate us at some point and that we'd be assigned to different detachments; maybe we were only together for a little while. For months I wanted to ask how you felt about that, but I didn't dare to."

"Why?"

"I was afraid of what the answer might be. I didn't know what your priorities were. If duty had called you far away, would you've been up and ready to leave, to protect and serve your fellow man? What did family duty mean to you at that point? Did you think of me as family? Perhaps I was only some bastard half-sibling to you."

"Heidi, I never treated you that way."

"No, but I didn't know what to expect then. We'd just met."

Jasper grew quiet, and all I could hear was his breathing. I believe the word "duty" had given him a forceful jolt.

"Are you angry?" I asked.

"No, it's a good question."

He said no more. I didn't understand what he was driving at, but I let it go and opened the window as I could hear music coming from the lodge beyond.

"Is that bagpipe?"

"I believe so."

At this moment, the lodge door opened and some fifteen men started marching out, gathering around the small building for casual conversation. We immediately recognized many of the visitors we'd met downtown earlier that day. Constable Winston stood out from the crowd adorned in red serge and masonic regalia.

Jasper frowned.

"He has no business wearing the uniform to perform these rites," he said.

"Look!"

Gordon Miller had just exited the lodge. He wore a heavy chain collar with a conspicuous pendant representing the square part of the masonic insignia. I'm no expert, but I suppose that means he's a big shot at the lodge. Miller approached Winston, and the men exchanged a warm handshake. They were chatting away when I noticed a familiar face among the group.

"Isn't that Simon Hall?" I asked.

I pointed and Jasper got a closer look using his binoculars.

"You're right... What do you think that means?"

"I don't know, but it stinks."

Simon Hall was my former husband's employer. He is the founder of Hall Insurance Brokers Limited. His business is believed to be a front for a lucrative drug operation in the Mackenzie Delta, but we never managed to gather enough evidence to put him away as is often the case with powerful men who excel in the art of dissimulation. Jasper had brought a camera. He turned the flash off and succeeded in taking a picture of the gathered Masons unnoticed. We quietly drove away to the detachment where we had his photograph printed out in a large format. Only then did we recognize another familiar face, that of Judge

Philip Meyer standing a few steps away from Hall and taking an active part in the conversation.

We presented our findings to our sergeant the following morning. When Inuvik's masonic lodge building had been inaugurated in 2004, Sergeant Matthews had welcomed the news very coldly. He had also refused to eat from the barbecued pig the Masons had offered our detachment a year earlier. We knew he would lend an open ear and take our concerns seriously.

"It was only a matter of time," he muttered after hearing us out and taking a long look at Jasper's photograph.

"You knew about this?"

"I know about the oaths of Freemasonry. You would like to think these occultists wouldn't venture this far out above the treeline, but no. They're everywhere."

Sergeant Matthews started rubbing his red moustache nervously. He had turned pale the way you would if you were to meet a doctor about a possible cancer diagnosis.

"Who else knows you're investigating this?"

"We did share some of this information with Corporal Alunik privately," I replied. "He already had his suspicions about the defense lawyer and had often witnessed his ring-tapping antics in the courtroom."

I believe the best word to describe Sergeant Matthew's expression at this point is dread. Looking back, I believe he was fully aware of the mountain he was asked to climb and was coming to terms with the likely consequences of fighting the battle.

"I will need you to be very quiet about this," he said.

We nodded and went about our usual business. In the meantime, Sergeant Matthews wrote a memorandum to the territory's Commanding Officer, which read as follows:

> It has come to my attention that Constable Frank Winston, who was transferred to this detachment in April 2005, is an active member of Inuvik's masonic lodge and has recently covered the crime of fellow Mason Gordon Miller, a local defense attorney we've often had contact with through the Territorial Court. Mr. Miller's impaired driving caused a collision on August 20, which left the other driver injured, but Constable Winston's report asserted that unfavourable weather was to blame for the road accident. A complaint lodged by the injured driver led Constables Jasper Nelson and Heidi Finlay to find clear weather conditions on August 20.
>
> Winston also failed to subject Mr. Miller to the breathalyzer test. Further investigation revealed both men's allegiance to the Masonic Order and active participation in the Inuvik lodge's last meeting held on September 11 (see photographic evidence below). Constable Winston wearing the red serge while partaking in masonic rituals is in clear contravention to RCMP regulations regarding the uniform and sends a problematic message of partiality to the lodge. Our Oath of Office does demand that

we 'perform all lawful orders and instructions without fear, favour or affection of or toward any person.'

In addition, Mr. Miller has often been seen gesturing to Judge Philip Meyer in court, indicating his masonic ring, a habit reported by three members at this detachment. Judge Meyer attended the meeting on September 11. These gestures have often resulted in Mr. Miller obtaining unusual success in the courtroom, contrary to the evidence and merits of the case. These cases are almost exclusively linked to bootlegging and drug operations in which Hall Insurance Brokers Ltd founder Simon Hall is suspected of taking part. Hall was also seen at the masonic meeting. I respectfully request this information be examined and action taken to halt the spread of this corruption.

Regards,
Sergeant Nathaniel Matthews
Inuvik RCMP

Considering the scope of allegations our case presented, we did not expect prompt action on our superiors' part, but prepared to wait patiently, knowing we had done our duty by shedding light on the secretive order and its reprehensible methods. We were rather surprised to have Sergeant Matthews call us into his office the following morning. Our sergeant had already received a curt response from Staff

Sergeant Major Henry Moore on behalf of the Northwest
Territories' Commanding Officer:

Dear Sergeant Matthews,

We have examined your query regarding con-
nections between the Masonic Lodge, Royal
Canadian Mounted Police and the judiciary.
We would like to inform you that your memorandum has been destroyed. Be assured that
disciplinary measures will be taken should you
investigate further or interfere with the Inuvik
Lodge's activities. These wild speculations are
preposterous. We ask that this investigation
be closed and your meddlesome constables
notified. As you may well know, Masonry has
played an important part in RCMP history,
helping us become the illustrious Force that we
are today. Focus on that which falls within your
competence. 'Dwell in the land, serve the king
of Babylon, and it shall be well with you.'

Cordially yours,
Staff Sergeant Major Henry Moore

The note left us speechless. My heart was racing. Was it
from anger? From fear? Perhaps it was the realization that
our Staff Sergeant Major was a twisted despot with little
regard for the rule of law.

"Is this man a Mason himself?" Jasper inquired.

"He is. I was able to confirm it by speaking to a colleague who knows him well. He told me he once came across Moore's masonic regalia in his office."

"What does this have to do with the king of Babylon?" I asked.

"I believe it's a biblical reference," Jasper replied.

"It is. It almost sounds like they are associating themselves with the idea of Babylon."

"What do you think it means?"

"Babylon was an idolatrous kingdom the Israelites were deported to after falling into idolatry themselves. Under Babylonian rule, they learned to appreciate the God-given law they had despised in their own country."

"Is this verse used in masonic rites?"

"I don't know. I suppose it's Moore's way of reminding us we are not in control."

"And he's calling *us* meddlesome?"

"We will not be silenced, Finlay. I have no intention of serving the king of Babylon. I'm going higher."

Sergeant Matthews' initial apprehension had turned into holy wrath. He proceeded to contact another commissioned officer, but I never knew the details of that communication. Corporal Alunik told us Winston had been called into Sergeant Matthews' office later that morning and confronted about his actions.

JASPER AND I were on highway patrol two days later when we received a call from Corporal Alunik who'd been tipped about a bootlegging operation underway near the Mike Zubko Airport. An anonymous female caller had described a black pick-up truck parked in a clearing along the Dempster Highway; two men were standing outside, and the back of the vehicle was filled with suspicious merchandise. She felt the RCMP should investigate it. We happened to be heading back to town near the end of our shift. Jasper was driving and pushed the pedal to the floor. I remember the excitement and the hope that we might just catch some of Simon Hall's gofers and find the key to bringing down his scheme.

We soon reached the clearing. There was no sign of life save the aforementioned black pick-up truck parked by the side of the road. We examined our surroundings and stepped out of the vehicle, pistol ready. It is difficult to explain what happened next because everything became a blur. A young man armed with a semi-automatic rifle bounced out of a ditch behind us and discharged a hail of bullets before we even had a chance to notice his presence. We both fell face first to the ground. Oddly enough, my first impression was that a wild animal had pushed me and stepped all over my body. The sensation soon turned to burning. The last things I remember are the masked shooter driving away and Jasper calling for help on his radio. He then cried out to me in panic. I extended my hand to him, but I must have passed out after this.

The tip had let us straight into Hall's ambush; he'd likely obtained his information from Constable Winston. I suppose the clearing had been selected because it is far enough from town, and we were expected to bleed to death before anyone came to our rescue. Jasper's vague cry was fortunately picked up by Corporal Alunik who got things moving and sent an ambulance to get us. A doctor later explained we were both in hypovolemic shock by the time we were admitted to the emergency room. The bullet-proof vests had protected our vital organs, but our backs were covered in nasty bruises, and our arms and legs had been hit or grazed in several places. My brother took four bullets and I took five. We were in and out of consciousness for hours, and the powerful medication kept us in a haze for days. We were then moved out of intensive care and hospital personnel were kind enough to put us in the same room. Sarah and her daughter visited one evening, and Aluki cried the whole time. She stood far from the bed as if she were afraid to touch and hurt me. None of our colleagues dropped by during that time, and we were unaware of what was happening at the detachment. Sarah seemed to know something was amiss, but she kept quiet so as not to upset us in our convalescence.

Ruben Alunik showed up the next day. We smiled and greeted him cheerfully. We tried to sit up, squirming to find a decent position and avoid lying on the wounds covering our bodies. Under different circumstances, Alunik might have cracked a joke at our expense, but he wasn't laughing at all now.

"Look at you," he muttered. "He shot you in the back and scampered away like a coward. Did you get a chance to see his face or license plate?"

Jasper shook his head.

"He wore a ski mask. The plate had been removed. The operation was meticulously planned."

Corporal Alunik stared at the floor for some time. He admitted he had really come to bid us goodbye. He announced he was being transferred to the Paulatuk detachment, 400 kilometres northeast of Inuvik. The decision was not his.

My heart sank.

"What about Sergeant Matthews?" I asked.

"Sergeant Matthews took a flight back to Saskatchewan with his family early this morning. Seized cocaine taken from an exhibit was found in his car on Monday. The way I understand it, he was told he wouldn't face charges if he resigned and he did... That cocaine was definitely planted. You and I know Matthews wouldn't be caught dead with illicit substances in his possession. He knows too much, and they want him out of the way."

"He simply agreed to resign? He didn't even try to defend himself?"

"I believe he was threatened. Perhaps he feared for his wife and children. The media are doing their best to tarnish his reputation. Worst is that lots of folks are buying it and most will only hear the lies and never know the truth. Winston probably had a hand in all of it, but it'll be impossible to prove and they'll cover for him anyway. They've taken oaths."

The world suddenly felt like such an absurd place that I wished those bullets had snuffed me out after all.

"He asked me to give you this," Alunik said.

He handed me a get-well card in which Sergeant Matthews had written:

> Do not lose heart, Finlay. 'Greater is he that is
> in you, than he that is in the world.' (1 John 4:4)

> Nathaniel Matthews

I remembered the verse from a sermon I'd heard at the Baptist church a few weeks before. I would attend once in a while with Sergeant Matthews and his family when I didn't have to work on Sunday. I could see the relevance of it, but it provided little comfort at the moment.

"This is beyond me," Jasper murmured.

"I suppose they'd been keeping their eye on us since we investigated Hall after Duncan disappeared ten years ago. It goes all the way back, Heidi."

"You think Duncan was involved?"

"Hard to say. I don't know how much he knew. Constant contact with the underworld probably encouraged his vice. What could have led to his meltdown? Was he running from them? Who knows?"

"If he was running, he left Heidi in a vulnerable position."

"Indeed... I made some calls. I spoke to a retired sergeant major in BC who's been looking into masonic influence for some time. He was interested in hearing our story."

Did you ever find yourself at the foot of a mountain where the very effort of looking up to the peak gave you vertigo? I think this is how my brother felt inside right then.

"It goes way up, Nelson. Way higher than you think."

"Meaning?"

"A quarter of our prime ministers were known Masons. From the very beginning. John A. MacDonald, John Abbott, Bowell, Borden, Bennett, even good old Diefenbaker... Makes you question a bunch of things, doesn't it? MacDonald introduced the residential school system. He starved scores of Aboriginal people down south. Was that part of an elite's sinister plan to control things?"

We were silent for a long time. Alunik laid his coat on a chair and sat on my bed. I felt the mattress sink under his giant mass.

"I think you two should lay low for a while."

"I'm going back to the bush, anyway," I said.

"Are you resigning?"

"We're both resigning," Jasper replied.

Alunik turned to my brother in shock.

"You too, Nelson? I expected more tenacity on your part."

Jasper looked away. I could tell he was getting emotional. Alunik made it sound like he was giving up and acting selfishly. I believe it was shame he was feeling. In fact, we both felt humiliated. Why, you will ask, if we had worked to denounce corruption and walk the straight and narrow? I cannot explain it. Perhaps it is the way our adversaries had scorned our efforts and riposted with violence and dishonesty. I suppose intimidation goes hand in hand with dishonour.

"I have a duty to look after my own," Jasper answered. "I don't want Heidi to get killed. I don't want to die and leave her alone, either. There are other ways to uphold the right."

Alunik nodded.

"I'm with you. But I need to stay for my people's sake. To make sure the Inuvialuit get a fair treatment and their needs are met."

"We understand, Ruben."

I pressed his hand and began to tear up. I didn't want him to go and wondered how many good things were left in my life at this point.

WE WERE IN the hospital for two weeks. Jasper had to use a cane for a month after that due to the considerable damage done to his right leg. I had only sustained grazes and flesh wounds. We retreated to my cabin in the bush. Once I could get around, I began setting rabbit snares to add some meat to the beans, flour and dry fruit we'd stored away in our cache. I also had moose round left from a young bull I'd shot in September. Jasper could not walk much, so I looked after him. He felt awful about it and I constantly had to remind him I was glad to do it. Jasper had not shaved while in the hospital and decided to let his hair and beard grow, feeling it might make him harder to identify if there was a prize on his head. We had sufficient ground to believe there was. It made him look unkempt for a while. I sensed an identity crisis within him, as he could no longer think of himself as the valiant constable he'd once been and was figuring out what was left of him without the red serge. I began noticing signs of depression. One night, I heard him cry "Dear God!" and there was some sobbing. I did not intervene, as it sounded as if he might be praying. I had never seen or heard my brother pray before, but darker times can make us seek help higher up, as I have witnessed and experienced myself. The most reputable human establishments had failed him. Who could he now trust and look to for meaning and a desire to live?

Living in the bush keeps you busy since you do not have access to the facilities they have in town. Washing clothes by hand, cooking and getting the stove going would help me avoid anxiety and reconsidering my decision to quit. But my brother's injury forced him to sit and brood all day. I too would feel the gloom when evening came and the chores were done. We would often go to bed with fear in our hearts and our Winchester rifle close at hand. We had brought a fold-up mattress we'd spread out by the stove and set our sleeping bags side by side. We huddled together and managed to get some sleep that way.

This time spent in the bush with my brother would have been wonderful if it hadn't happened in this trying context. As much as we feared for our safety and wondered what life had in store for us after this, we were relieved and allowed to rest in a way that had not been possible for years. Constables are exposed to human depravity every single day; keeping your sanity can be a challenge sometimes. I'd been wanting out for a while, but Jasper Nelson's idealism kept him hoping and kept me going. He inspired me to persevere. I felt lost when he chose to resign too because I thought he had sunk into cynicism, which is the last thing you would expect of a man like him.

After a month's time, we presumed Simon Hall and his underlings were satisfied with our resignation and would not insist on wiping my brother and I off the face of the earth.


SARAH KUDLAK DROPPED by for a visit the other day and brought us fresh fruits and vegetables. I know she has been cutting her husband's hair for years and asked if she could give both my brother and I a trim. I got a bob cut, which is quite a change because I always needed to keep my hair long enough to tie it back when I was a constable. Jasper's beard makes him look much older, not so much in years as in wisdom, and there was something of a sage in his countenance once Sarah was done combing and cleaning him up.

"You look quite handsome like this," I told him later that night.

"I'm a tired old man," he replied with a grin.

"Don't say that. You're a noble man."

The compliment made him look down, as if he felt he did not deserve it. His attitude had been serene in the last few days, but this seemed to make him slip back into confusion.

"Do you regret your decision?" I asked, frankly.

"Do you?"

"At times."

"Was it a decision or an obligation?"

"It sure felt like an obligation at the time. Do you think Sergeant Matthews would approve? Or he'd think we ran like deserters?"

"Hard to say. It would have been reckless to persist. At the end of the day, I know I refused to make a mistake I have made several times before. *That* was a decision."

"What mistake?"

"Putting the Force first. Neglecting my own. It made me lonely for years; it would have been senseless to keep doing the same thing."

"You want to keep us safe?"

"I don't want us putting our lives on the line anymore. The Force is crooked. We can provide all the evidence in the world, but it's never enough to condemn those with special privilege or protection."

"You need to stop mulling over this. Let you mind rest."

"I've rested enough already," Jasper declared, picking up a folder from the coffee table. "I plan to go to the press. Get in touch with Nathaniel Matthews and that retired officer Alunik spoke of."

Jasper told me he had made a copy of all documents pertaining to the recent events. He'd just begun leafing through them after keeping them away until the storm abated.

"Be careful. Journalists often get the story twisted," I said.

"We'll find an objective one."

"Good luck."

"I'll write it myself."

"Those elites are pulling the strings. We'll be labelled as conspiracy theorists."

"We can't hold the truth in unrighteousness."

"No, we can't."

I smiled as I could see my brother had not lost his resolve. He is seeking an alternative way of letting the truth out. Jasper is considering a new career in investigative journalism, thinking he can bring an interesting perspective to the *Inuvik Drum's* crime news section. I no longer look to man to find my bearings in life, but it is heartening to see wholesome folks working to make justice happen down here once in a while. Knowing Jasper Nelson is still out to get his man helps take the sting out of this injury.

We recently ventured into town and learned from Sarah that Ann Nasogaluak dropped her complaint after an envelope containing $10,000 and a short letter asking her to do so was left in her mailbox. The letter had no signatory. She didn't quite know what to do, but chose to take the money and keep her mouth shut, especially after hearing there had been an attempt on our lives for trying to help her. Ruben Alunik had left a message on my answering machine, asking how we were. We called back and found out Constable Winston had been promoted to Corporal and had been transferred to Alberta where he now runs his own detachment. We were appalled, but also reassured to know he was no longer living in Inuvik.

Jasper says we should take some time off in the spring and travel to British Columbia where he once promised to take me. He would like to find Duncan and shed some light on his hasty flight ten years ago. He thinks he could provide intelligence on Simon Hall's shady dealings. I don't really like the sound of this, but if Jasper takes the lead, I think I could handle it.

Jasper is staying in town for a few days, and I am back in the bush harvesting and preparing my pelts for the January auction. I don't believe I have lost my touch. There are fox and marten furs hanging all around the cabin, and Jasper says the smell is "quite robust". It brings me back to my youth and what we like to call "simpler times". But times are never simple, only covered by many veils that come off one after another as we grow older and see the world for what it really is. But that is enough writing and contemplation for now, my traps need inspecting, and daylight is already fading on the black spruce beyond.

CPSIA information can be obtained
at www.ICGtesting.com
Printed in the USA
LVHW090615071219
639732LV00001B/29/P